# Finding Forever

Jarka,

happy reading

Amanda J. [signature]

Also by Amanda J Evans and coming in 2017

Save Her Soul

# Finding Forever

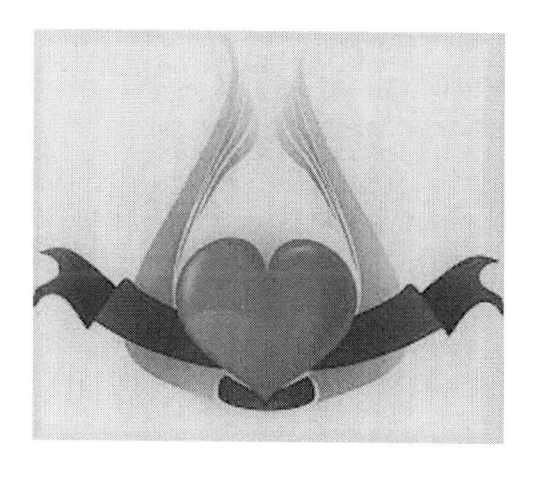

AMANDA J EVANS

Copyright © 2017 Amanda J Evans

All rights reserved. This book or parts thereof may not be reproduced in any form, stored in any retrieval system, or transmitted in any form by any means—electronic, mechanical, photocopy, recording, or otherwise—without prior written permission of the author.

This is a work of fiction. Names, characters, places, and incidents either are the products of the author's imagination or are used fictitiously. Any resemblance to actual persons, living or dead, businesses, companies, events, or locales is entirely coincidental.

Visit the author's website at www.amandajevans.com.

Cover Design: Lee Ching – Under Cover Designs

First Edition

ISBN: 1542360161
ISBN-13: 978-1542360166

# DEDICATION

For all those who believe love is worth fighting for. This book is for you as a reminder to never give up on finding your forever.

For my husband Joe and my children Emma and Conor who believed in my dream and encouraged me to never give up

# ACKNOWLEDGMENTS

I would like to thank all the amazing beta readers who read my story and provided the feedback required to complete the manuscript. Thank you all for your kind words and your excitement for this book. To Lee from Under Cover Designs: Book Cover, my amazing cover designer, thank you for your wonderful book cover. To Lynda Kirby, my good friend and editor, thank you for all your help during the editing phase. To Caroline Connolly and Maria B Bourke, thank you for your friendship and encouragement and your comments on my story. This wouldn't have happened without you all.

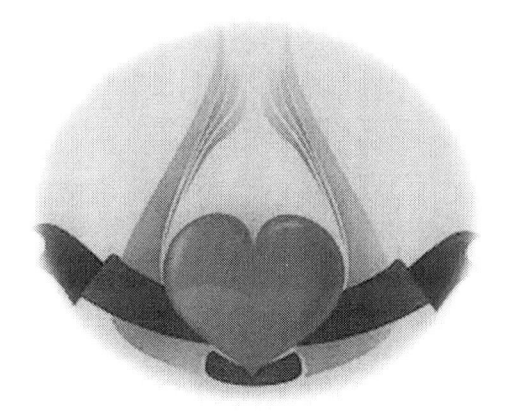

## **LIZ**

The sun was high in the sky when I opened my eyes. I felt the heat burning the back of my neck, the red blush noticeable on my arms. I should have been enjoying my surroundings, the palm trees, white sand, and the sound of birds chirping. I thought of the pink bikini I'd packed, the sunbathing, and the memories we would create. I banished them just as quickly as I sat motionless staring out at the deep blue sea. I always loved the sea, the peace, and the tranquility it brought. I hadn't planned on it being the last thing I would see, though. Yesterday was the best day of my life. The perfect wedding, white and luxurious just as we'd planned it. I truly believed that my life was just beginning when we boarded Charles' yacht with friends and family for our wedding reception. It was everything I'd ever imagined, the sun, the sea, the laughter, the champagne. My lips tilted into a smile as I remembered dancing on the deck, soft, romantic music filling the air and night lanterns setting the tone. I thought of the smiles and memorable moments our photographer captured. I'd never see them now.

How quickly perfection can fade. Just one moment is all it takes and for me, that moment decided to freeze. I was locked inside the trauma. I tried pinching myself awake, convinced I was trapped in a nightmare, suffering from wedding nerves. It happened so many times over the past week, night terrors, screams, sweat dripping, and heart racing, all ending with me bolting upright, at home, in my bed. It didn't happen this time and as my eyes took in the tattered remains of my Armani wedding dress, I knew this was a nightmare I wasn't escaping from.

No one ever tells you what happens when a body dies. They don't tell you about what happens next. I heard death had a distinctive smell, but the putrid rotting that was filling my nostrils was something I could never have prepared myself for. I knew I needed to move, to cover the body, something, but I was paralyzed. I sat holding Charles' hand. It was so cold now, but I couldn't move. I couldn't leave his side. Till death do us part…. the words played on repeat inside my mind, and besides, I promised I would wake him as soon as the rescue party arrived. He was so tired from the swimming, so. He tried to stay awake. He really did, but sleep took him. I don't know when death arrived, one minute his chest was heaving in and out, a wheezing sound filling the night. It gave me comfort. I knew he was still with me. I don't know when I passed out, I just know I did and when I woke there was silence. I tried to wake him, I shook his limp body but I guess I knew deep down he had lost the battle so I just sat here holding his hand, praying that I was wrong, that he would come back to me. I wouldn't let my vows go, I wouldn't.

The sun was getting hotter and I knew my skin was burning, but I didn't care. We picked the perfect honeymoon location, a small tropical island, secluded, and private. It was just what we needed, two weeks of married bliss wrapped up in our own little bubble. No one would be looking for us, no one. I curled up against Charles and wept. There was nothing for me to do now but wait for death to come and take me too.

My eyes fluttered open. I'd fallen asleep. My legs were sore and aching. I needed to move, to find shade. I looked out to sea once more. My vision was blurred and I knew the sun was starting to get to me. I blinked forcing my focus as a ship came into view. A large schooner was there. I shook my head. I was imagining things. This was the fifth time I had imagined a ship, although nothing like this. Then I saw them, four little boats heading to the shore. I closed my eyes and opened them slowly. It was still there, the ship, and the boats were getting closer. My heart rate increased. The rescue party was here; they were coming to get us.

"Charles, Charles, they're here, they're coming, we're being rescued."

"Charles," the word evaporated on the wind and my body crumpled as sobs took over. He wasn't going to wake up. He wasn't going to be rescued. I looked back to the sea and the boats that were getting closer.

"It's only me," I whispered.

I kissed Charles on the head, my tears flowing down his face, and I forced myself move. My body was stiff and didn't want to cooperate, but I knew I had to be ready to leave my nightmare and begin a new one, life as a widow.

The boats arrived quicker than I thought they would and

as I watched, hidden behind the trees, I realized this wasn't my rescue party. They weren't looking for me. No, they were here for something else and it had nothing to do with being tourists.

Rough looking bearded men stepped onto the beach. I gasped as I watched numerous sets of strong legs clad in torn trousers step onto the sand. They all had thick long arms and were armed with weapons. Grizzled stubble and lips twisted into sneers and grimaces finished their appearance. I was grateful they didn't see me. I crept further behind the line of palm trees. It wasn't a great hiding place, but it was better than nothing. I watched them scan the beach.

"Fucking hell John, what happened here?" "Looks like we missed one hell of a party," one of them yelled.

I watched them walk towards the scattered wreckage washed up on the shore, stop and then start rummaging through it.

"Ah hell," I heard another voice coming from my left. "There's nothing here, just wreckage, must've been a fine vessel, though."

They inspected the broken pieces of our yacht that had washed ashore. I was hidden, they couldn't see me. I was safe. They walked up and down the beach checking through the remains, picking up bits and pieces and putting them in their pockets.

"Look here, look what I've found," another voice shouted.

I looked around the tree. One of the men was bent over Charles holding up his grandfather's gold watch.

"It's solid gold and look here, a solid gold ring to go with it"

His grin stretched from ear to ear and I snapped. That was my Charles, how dare they.

"Get your hands off him," I screamed as I shot out from behind the trees.

My scream obviously startled them because I looked up to find eight, big burly men staring back at me.

"You leave him alone do you hear me," I continued.

My tears fell as I raced over to where Charles lay. So, pale and still. I started shaking him. "Baby it's me, you can wake up now. We've been rescued."

He didn't move. I kept shaking, and shaking, and shaking, but it wasn't working.

"Come on now missy, he ain't gonna wake, he's gone."

I heard the voice over my head but I wasn't listening. My mind was blank. My body was stiff. My hands gripped the collar of Charles shirt as I shook him. He wouldn't wake. He couldn't wake. He really had left me. The realization hit me and everything went blank. Nothing worked and nothing was real anymore. Grief took over.

"Come on missy, we'll take you to the ship. The captain will know what to do."

I felt hands lift me but I didn't care. I didn't care about anything now. Let them take me. Let them do what they like. My life was over.

\*\*\*

My eyes opened. My head was pounding and my vision was blurred. I blinked a few times.

"What happened?" My voice was croaky and my throat hurt. I tried to sit up but I was dizzy. I blinked again as my eyes adjusted and I took in my surroundings. I was in a dark wooden room. It was small, dark, and it smelled of damp and sea water. I looked down. I was in a small bunk bed. The smell was coming from the old woolen blanket that was thrown over me. I threw it to the floor and swung my legs over the side of the bed. My body swayed as I tried to gain my footing. There was a mirror on the far wall. My mind was running in circles. What had happened? Memories of the beach, Charles' cold, lifeless body, and men.

"Oh fuck, those men. What had they done to me?"

As the reality of my situation dawned I realized the swaying motion wasn't me. The whole room was moving. I was moving. I was on their ship. I was at sea…. again.

I made my way across to the mirror and braced myself for what I was about to see. I took a deep breath and lifted my head shocked at what was looking back at me. My beautiful dark curls were now matted and a dark red color. I moved it away from my forehead. There was a large gash in my hairline. That was where the blood covering my face must have come from. It was still weeping, but nothing much. I wiped it away with the back of my hand relieved that it didn't reappear instantly. I knew the cut needed stitches but it was probably too late for that now. The skin was knitting back together. I sighed as I looked closely at the woman reflected in the mirror. My face was unrecognizable. Gone was the beautiful makeup, gone was the stunning bride that greeted me yesterday morning. Instead, I found myself looking into black, desolate eyes. My normal green sparkling eyes had faded, filled with grief. My tanned skin now looked grayish and completed the look of utter bewilderment. I didn't look like me. I looked……lost.

I noticed a glass of water reflected in the mirror and realized that my throat was on fire. I gulped it down in one but it wasn't enough. My body was craving more, it needed more. I looked around, I was going to have to leave this room. I was nervous. I didn't know why. These were my rescuers, the people who had saved me. They were going to help me.

More like captors, my mind screamed as I placed my hand on the door knob. Easing it open, I peered out onto the deck. It was quiet and the moon was high in the sky. Had I slept all day? I looked around taking in the ship that had saved me. I could hear the sails flapping and rustling, the mast creaking as the breeze pushed through the sails. The deck was dark the only light coming from a cabin at the far end. I let my eyes adjust to the darkness while I looked around, and then I saw it. Like a demon, risen high on the mast, the thing of nightmares, of destruction. A large black flag bearing a skull and crossbones. I hadn't been rescued at all. I had been captured by pirates and I realized in that moment that my life really had ended on the beach with Charles.

*Wait a minute, pirates don't exist do they? This isn't real, it can't be.*

I froze, my hand against the wooden door. My body began to shake and my feet felt stuck to the floor. I had no idea what was happening, why I was here, or who these people were.

*You have to move, get off this ship.*

My body refused to listen. My mind screamed at me to move again and my body came to life. I peered out of the gap in the door once more. The deck looked empty and everything was quiet. I eased myself through the door, pulling it behind me as softly as I could. Not soft enough though because it creaked loudly. Before I could move there was a man in front of me. I swallowed hard as I looked up at him. He was tall. Long legs made their way up to a thick middle and strong chest with hair sticking out above the top of his t-shirt. My eyes moved higher and I was greeted with a crooked grin and dark eyes.

"Ah you're awake, Captain's waiting to see you, lassie."

"I…I.." My voice failed me and I started coughing. My throat was burning and I needed water.

"Come on lass, let's get you to the captain and sort you out with some water. You sound like you could do with some and there's no telling how long you were out there on that beach."

Without waiting for me to reply, he clasped his hand around my arm and led me towards the other side of the boat. We stopped in front of a large door and he started banging.

"The ladies awake captain. Should I bring her in?"

"Aye do Jacobs," came a voice from behind the door.

My stomach heaved and my legs began to shake as panic took over my body.

"Don't worry lass, he doesn't bite our captain. He's quite the ladies' man really."

My captor laughed as he shoved me through the door, shutting it behind me. The force of his push coupled with the fact that my legs weren't functioning properly landed me face first down on the floor. I raised my head and found myself looking at dark brown boots. A hand was thrust in front of my face followed by a smooth masculine voice.

"Here miss, let me help you to your feet, not gotten your sea legs yet I see."

I took the large hand and allowed him to help me to my feet and over to a small couch in the center of the room. It was soft and welcoming and I felt my body sink into it. I looked around, taking in my surroundings. I was in a small cabin. There was a wooden desk in front of me, bookshelves to the right, a small round window to the left, and wood everywhere.

"Some water miss?"

His voice brought me out of my daze and I offered my thanks as I took the glass and downed the cool liquid in one.

"More," I said holding out the empty glass.

The fog in my mind started to clear ever so slightly. I was obviously dehydrated. I looked up at this so-called Captain. He wasn't old, probably mid 40's with dark hair and a beard. He was well built with muscular arms and shoulders. He wouldn't be easy to escape from, not in my condition anyway. I felt my shoulders slump. What was the point in even thinking about escaping when I was at sea and god knows where? The shock of it all was taking its toll on me and my body started shaking again. I couldn't help it, pictures of my wedding, Charles with his piercing blue eyes, our vows, dancing, laughter, and then his cold lifeless body. My throat closed, my breathing heavy as I tried to gain control. I couldn't do this not now. I couldn't fall apart when I didn't know where I was. I had to concentrate on my escape. I would have plenty of time to fall apart later.

"Miss, your water."

I took the glass; my hands were shaking. I felt the cool water slip down my throat as I took another long drink. I needed to pull myself together. I lifted my head and looked into the eyes of the man in front of me. He looked confused, his hand gripping his chin as he stared back at me.

"You're shaking, let me get you a blanket. First time at sea I take it?" he said as he draped a woolen blanket over my shoulders. "Jacobs said you were in a terrible state on the beach, never seen such a good performance before."

"Performance?" *What was he on about?*

"Yes, it's okay miss, there're no cameras in here. This cabin is off limits. You can drop the act now. Although, I must say I am impressed. Where did they find you? We weren't expecting it, but that's the thing with reality shows isn't it. The producers said there'd be surprises thrown in when we least expected them. That's why we're all in character all the time.

Except in here though, this is the only room without cameras. The boys only went to the beach to check it out for a scavenger hunt planned for later in the week, the producers must have thought it would be a good way to surprise us. I must say, it worked out really well. Your acting skills are fantastic. Where did you study?"

I had absolutely no idea what this man was going on about. His words swirled around in my brain making no sense at all. Acting, cameras, reality show. This was utter nonsense. What about my Charles? My head was throbbing. Nothing made sense anymore. I couldn't control the panic that took over. I couldn't catch my breath, Charles' face was all I could see. His lifeless blue eyes staring up at me.

"Charles, what did you do with him?" I managed to splutter.

The captain looked at me confused. "Who's Charles?"

Those two words were all it took for my world to crumble once more. Charles was my everything, my world, and these men, these savages had picked over his body like he was a bounty they were claiming. My Charles lying there on the beach, waiting for me to wake him. I promised I would as soon as I saw the rescue boats. I promised.

I couldn't hold back the sobs that spilled from my shaking body. My ears started to ring and my vision was blurred. I felt myself slipping away.

"Get a doctor"

The sound reverberated in my ears as darkness filled the space around me and I let myself go.

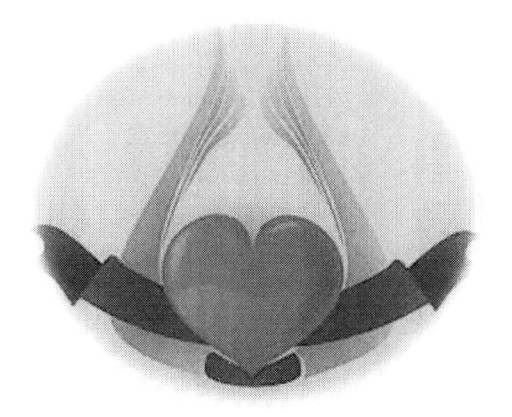

# LIZ

A bright light shining in my eyes woke me. I blinked trying to focus. My head was fuzzy and I couldn't see properly. After a few moments, I realized I wasn't moving anymore. I tried to sit up but the throbbing in my head made it impossible. I reached my hand up and felt bandages. Where was I? What had happened? My vision cleared and I looked to my left. There was a man sitting there slumped in a chair. The same man who had been on the ship, the one called the captain.

The sound of someone clearing their throat caught my attention and I looked up to see a doctor standing over me.

"Hello miss, I'm Doctor Phillips. It seems you've been through quite an ordeal; can you remember anything?"

I thought for a second, my head hurt and my memories felt a little jumbled, like pictures but not in the right sequence.

"Where's Charles?" I blurted out.

He was the most important thing. I needed to know what happened to him. Where was his body? Had those men left him to rot on the beach?

"Ah yes, Charles, John said you kept talking about someone called Charles." The doctor looked confused but his eyes carried a look of deep sympathy.

"Charles, my husband. He was with me on the beach. He was… he died." I spluttered as tears rolled down my cheeks. I could see him, my Charles, lying there on that beach, lifeless.

"I see." he nodded. "You've had a nasty blow to the head miss and you were quite dehydrated. We've run some tests but we're sure you're going to be just fine. I'm just going to get my colleague and then I'll be right back."

"But what about Charles?" I shouted.

Why was everyone avoiding answering my question? What had they done to him? This Doctor Phillips just looked at me, with pity in his eyes, shaking his head as he left the room. I heard movement from beside me and turned to see the captain staring at me.

"Where am I?" I asked.

"You're in the hospital miss, gave me an awful fright when you collapsed. I'm so sorry. I didn't realize."

"Didn't realize what?"

"Your injuries. I thought it was makeup, special effects. Once I realized you were really hurt we docked straight away and I brought you here."

"I don't understand. Why would you think it was makeup?" I asked confused.

None of this made any sense. My head was throbbing and

my heart ached. All I wanted was to find Charles, bury him, say goodbye, and then hide away from the world and slowly wither away into nothing. I had nothing left to live for now anyway.

"Miss, I told you, we're part of a documentary reality show on pirates. We were supposed to hunt for treasure on the island in a couple of days and the men were checking it out, but found you instead. You were in such a state and then you collapsed so they brought you back to the ship. We assumed you were an actress and you'd just had a little too much sun." He was shaking his head again. "I'm so sorry."

I didn't know what to make of all of this. My mind was still very fuzzy but I did remember the beach and those men standing over Charles. I remembered coming out from behind the trees screaming at them to leave him alone. I looked down at my hands. They were knotted tightly into the blankets that covered me. I couldn't stop the tears now as they fell from my cheeks. I looked up at this man and readied myself to ask the one question I was dreading.

"What did they do with Charles? Did they bring him back to the ship too?"

He looked at me with the same pity the doctor had shown, and gripped his chin. "There wasn't anyone else on the beach. Who is this Charles you keep asking about?"

"Charles, my husband." I blurted out. "He was with me on the beach, your men, they saw him, they had his grandfather's watch, and I jumped out, told them to leave him alone. They dragged me off his body."

I was shaking now, how could he not know what I was talking about. What the hell was going on here?

"Miss, you must be confused, there was no-one else on that beach, I assure you."

I snapped then, turning to him like a wild animal.

"WHAT DID YOU DO WITH MY HUSBAND?" I enunciated every word slowly but he just shook his head.

"I'm sorry miss, there wasn't anyone else on the beach."

"There was, Charles was there, he was.... he died in my arms."

I was sobbing now. Why was everyone lying to me? What was going on? Then I thought a little more. Perhaps those men didn't tell him about Charles. It helped a little and I took a deep breath before looking up at him once more.

"How far are we from the island?"

"What do you mean?"

"How far are we? I need to go back. I need to get Charles and bring him home. I can't leave him out there."

"We're not too far, but, I don't think that's a good idea. You're not well. The doc said you'll be here for a few days yet. They're running tests. You have a nasty gash on your head and you were severely dehydrated. You'll have to wait until you've been given the all clear before you can go anywhere."

"I have to get out of here," I said as the door to my room opened.

Dr. Phillips was back and this time he had another doctor with him.

"This is Doctor Andrews, a colleague, and friend. He'd like to have a word with you," he said motioning to the man at his side.

I looked at both gentlemen. "Okay."

"John, do you mind leaving us. We won't be long." Dr. Phillips said to the captain who began moving towards the door.

I was alone now with the two doctors and I had no idea what was going on.

"Hello, there. I'm Doctor Andrews. Do you mind if I take

a seat and we see if we can't get to the bottom of all this?"

He seemed nice and friendly. His hair was dark with gray patches around his temples. His eyes were soft and caring and I felt at ease. I nodded, giving my approval and he took the chair at the side of the bed.

"How about we start with your name?" He said smiling politely at me. "It's not filled in on the form," he said shuffling through the papers in his hands.

"Elizabeth, Elizabeth Parker," I said.

"Well Elizabeth, it's very nice to meet you. My name's Doctor Andrews but you can call me Mike."

I nodded once more. I wasn't feeling as anxious or nervous about talking to this Dr. Mike fellow. He seemed relaxed and he wasn't looking at me with eyes filled with pity like the other two men had.

"How about you tell me how it was you came to be a patient here in my hospital?"

He was holding a pen in his hand now, filling in the blanks on my hospital forms and probably getting ready to take notes.

"I don't really know," I started. "The last thing I remember is being on the ship in the captain's cabin and he was talking about cameras and I felt dizzy, and I was worried about Charles, and planning my escape, and then darkness, and I woke up here."

"That's quite a lot of information, Elizabeth, do you mind if we go back a little bit. What happened before you came to be on the ship? Do you remember that?"

I nodded, swallowing hard, and began to tell Dr. Andrews all about my wedding on board the Princess Elizabeth. Charles had named his yacht after me. I explained how we held our reception on the yacht with all our friends and Charles' family.

I told him about dancing and about how happy I was. He took notes while I spoke and glanced up every so often smiling and reassuring me. I felt at ease and I could feel my body beginning to relax for the first time since this ordeal began.

"Do you mind if I stop you for a moment, Elizabeth? You mention friends and Charles' family, but what about your own?"

"Oh," I frowned. "I don't have any family; my parents were killed in a car accident five years ago. It's just me now and Charles."

I could feel the tears filling my eyes but I refused to let them fall. I had to get through this story so that I could get out of here and find Charles. Dr. Andrews must have sensed my upset and decided to leave the questions about my family.

"So Elizabeth, let's go back to your wedding on the yacht. What happened after all your guests left? Do you think you can tell me about that?"

I felt my shoulders relax as I took a deep breath and began again.

"After our guests left Charles set a course for the island. We were going to spend our honeymoon there, just the two of us with no distractions."

"I see, and were you or Charles drunk when you set course for the island?"

"No, definitely not."

I was shocked that he would even ask such a question. Charles was a dedicated sailor there is no way he would risk such a thing.

"Charles had to stay sober to sail the yacht, so he didn't really have anything to drink, and I only had a glass or two of champagne. Why do you ask, do you think it was Charles' fault that the yacht sank? He was an excellent sailor, there is no way he would have done anything to put us in danger."

I was shaking now and I could feel myself getting angry. How dare he suggest Charles caused this? Charles loved me, he loved his boat. He would never have intentionally done anything wrong.

"I'm sorry, Elizabeth. I had to ask. Please go on. What happened next, tell me everything you remember?"

I cast my mind back to that night, back to the quiet of the yacht after everyone had left and began to tell the doctor.

"Charles and I had a glass of champagne to celebrate our future together. Then we sat and watched the sunset. Things get a little blurry after that." I explained. "I remember a loud bang, and cold water and Charles screaming and dragging me. I remember swimming, and then waking up on the beach."

Dr. Andrews was nodding his head at me again. "Elizabeth you received a very nasty blow to your head, but I still need to ask you something. Did Charles open the bottle of champagne that you said you had after your guests left?"

He was looking very serious now and I was getting worried.

"No, the caterers left it open in our cabin when they were leaving. Why are you asking me all of this? What has it got to do with anything?"

"We found drugs in your system, Ms. Parker, the type of drugs that would leave you with severe memory lapses. We need to determine where the drugs came from."

"Well, it wasn't Charles." I sobbed. "He loves me. We were going to spend the rest of our lives together."

I couldn't take anymore. My tears flowed freely now and I placed my head in my hands. I could feel my shoulders shaking as my sobs took over. How could he, how could he possibly think Charles would do this to me. Not my Charles. He was the gentlest man you could ever meet. He was kind and caring. He would never hurt anyone, especially not me. He loved me.

"I'm going to leave you for a while now. Let all the information I have just given you sink in. Hopefully, some additional memories will come back to you over the next couple of hours and we can get to the bottom of this mess." Dr. Andrews said as he stood over my bed.

"When can I leave?" I asked peering up at him.

"You've been through quite an ordeal and it's going to take time. We want to keep you in for observation but you should be free to go in a couple of days once your body has been fully rehydrated and your concussion clears. I'll be back to check on you later. You should get some rest and try to eat something. Breakfast is being served now, I'll get an attendant to bring you something."

He patted my hand and made his way out of the room. From the look on his face, I could tell he thought I was mad. I'd seen that look before. I knew how hospitals worked especially psychologists. I placed my head in my hands and let myself cry. I needed to. I had been holding it in for so long but I just couldn't do it anymore. Charles' face kept flashing in front of my eyes. My promise that I would wake him as soon as our rescue party arrived. I had broken my promise. I hadn't woken him. I hadn't tried hard enough. I should have woken him. I should have stayed by his side. It was all my fault that he was out there on that beach, alone. He needed me and I had to get back to him.

Moments later I heard someone clear their throat. I looked up and it was the captain.

*Why was he still here? What did he want from me? Did he think I was mad too?*

I looked into his eyes but all I saw was compassion. He

looked at me as if all he wanted to do was help.

"Sorry to disturb you miss. I just wanted to make sure you were okay. The doc said you were upset."

"Why are you here?" I asked looking up at him. His eyes were so caring and I felt safe in his presence but I didn't know what he wanted. I didn't know why he had stayed with me while I was unconscious.

"I couldn't leave without knowing that you were okay. I feel terrible. I should have gotten you to the hospital sooner. But you see, I thought you were an actress. I'm so sorry."

He was shaking his head and I knew he was being sincere.

"Do you know what happened to Charles?" I asked.

"I'm afraid I don't know who Charles is." He said looking confused.

So, I told him. I told him everything I could remember and he sat and he listened. He scratched his chin a few times and blew out a breath of air when I told him how I attacked the men on the beach when they took Charles' watch. He waited until I had finished before he cleared his throat. He was looking at me now with such sadness in his eyes and I saw the pity there too. I couldn't bear it. I turned my face away.

"I really don't know what's going on here miss, but you need to know Charles wasn't on that beach."

My head flew around and I met his eyes.

"He wasn't real. It was a dummy. That's why we thought you were an actress."

I opened my mouth but nothing came out.

*A dummy. Not real. What did he mean?*

"No, you're wrong. Charles was there. He was with me. He was breathing, and then…." I looked at this man, this captain, through my tears. "How could Charles be a dummy? I don't understand."

The captain straightened in the chair.

"It wasn't a real body miss, that's all I can tell you. I don't know what happened to your husband or what kind or ordeal you've been through. All I can tell you is that you were the only person on that beach, besides the dummy. I swear it."

I was frantic now. My head was throbbing. My memories were missing, and the ones I did have weren't real or so I was being told. I had to find Charles. I had to get to the bottom of this.

"How far away from the island are we? Can you take me back there? I promise I'm not mad. Charles was with me and I need to find him."

I watched his eyes glaze over. I needed him to believe me but he was shaking his head.

"I don't know about this. You've had a dreadful shock miss, and the doctors said you could be here for a few more days."

"I don't care what the doctors said." I snapped. "And for god's sake will you stop calling me miss. My name is Elizabeth."

He looked shocked at my outburst but he didn't say anything so I continued with my rant.

"I'm leaving this hospital now and going to that island whether you help me or not." I started to get out of the bed. My legs were a little unsteady and I stumbled. He reached out and grabbed my arm.

"Slow down miss, I mean Elizabeth. Let me help you."

I looked up at him. "Will you take me to the island? Will you help me find Charles?"

"I know I'm going to regret this but I hate seeing a woman upset. I'll help you in any way I can, but you have to listen to me and you have to let me help. Is that understood?"

"I promise I will," I said feeling a wave of relief wash over me. I was going back to the island. I was going to find my Charles.

I looked up at his face, this man John who had just promised to help me. His eyes held such sorrow and pain when he looked at me.

"Why are your helping me?"

"You remind me of someone I used to know." He said, his eyes glazing over as if caught in a memory.

"Someone special?"

"Very, my sister. She was treated here, in that very same bed."

"So that's how the doctor knew you. I had wondered about that. What happened to her?"

I was hoping I wasn't pushing too far with my nosy questions, but there was just something niggling in the back of my mind.

His shoulders slumped and I knew whatever it was, it was painful. I was about to tell him it didn't matter when he started talking.

"Susan was troubled. Delusions they said, split personality and so forth. She said someone was trying to kill her, someone evil. She was convinced but there was never any evidence. Doctors said it was all in her head. They kept her here for two months convinced her she was safe and that the medication they gave her would work."

He shook his head and lowered his eyes to the ground. "It didn't work, two days after her release she was found dead."

"I'm so sorry, what happened to her?"

"They ruled it as suicide but I just don't know, maybe there was someone after her, maybe they waited. I just don't know."

His grief and guilt were palpable and I could feel his pain.

"But you believe me, don't you? You believe that Charles was with me on that beach…I didn't just imagine him."

"I don't know whether to believe you or not, but I know one thing, and that is that I'll make damn sure I find out one way or another."

With this final statement, we made our way to the door.

"How are we going to get out of here?"

"You leave that to me. I'll talk to Doc Phillips; tell him we'll be back in 24 hours. He owes me, it's the least he can do. Now come on, we don't have any time to waste."

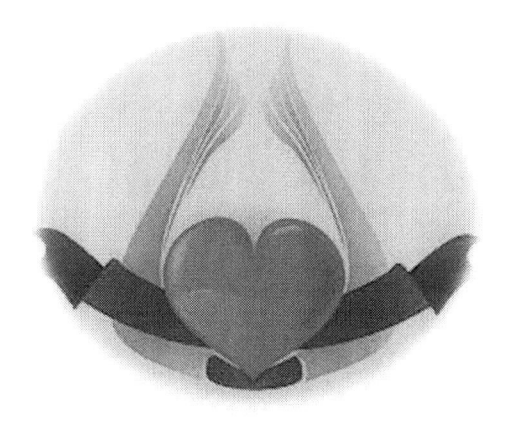

# CHARLES

My head pounded as I pried my eyes open.

"Ah, Charlie boy there you are. I was beginning to think I'd given you too much."

I turned my head towards the voice. My vision was out of focus and I could just make out a black shadow in front of me. I shook my head attempting to wake myself, clear my vision. It didn't do much good. Laughter sounded around me. I tried to move my arms only to realize they were bound behind my back.

"What the hell?"

"Now, now Charlie boy, we've plenty of time for questions. Let's wake you up first."

Without warning, water soaked my face and body, and quickly brought me back into full consciousness. I pulled my hands the rope or whatever was restraining me bit into my flesh and I felt the warm trickle of blood as it rolled down my wrists. I lashed out with my feet only to be greeted with the same sinister laughter. I looked up at my captor gritting my teeth as anger built. If this was some sick joke there'd be hell to pay.

"Who the fuck are you?" I snarled at the man in front of me. My vision had cleared thanks to the impromptu cold shower, but I didn't recognize him. He looked at me and smiled.

"I said, WHO THE FUCK ARE YOU?"

I was seething now and all this motherfucker could do was grin.

"Calm down Charlie boy, no point in upsetting yourself. We've a long way to go yet."

Bloody cryptic answers, a long way to go…where the hell was I? The last thing I remembered was…..

"Liz, where's Liz?"

"Ah, now you're remembering. I wouldn't worry about that pretty little wife of yours, she's most likely feeding all the seagulls and wildlife on the island now."

The island, oh god yes, our honeymoon, the yacht….it sank. My memories flooded back.

"If you've touched her I swear you'll pay."

I tried to lash out once more pulling on my bonds. The sharp sting of flesh tearing stopped me from doing any more damage.

"Tut, tut, Charlie boy, you're in no fit state to be making threats. I hold all the cards here. I'm in control, not you."

Who the hell was this man? I needed to get answers and

fast. I had to find out what happened to Liz and why I was tied up wherever I was. I looked around taking everything in. I was in a small room. It looked like some sort of shack. There was nothing in it. A dirty window was letting in some light, so I knew it was day time, and there was a chair in front of me, and a table in the corner of the room, but nothing else. I couldn't make out anything outside the window, not from my position on the floor anyway.

"So, Charlie boy, you recognize me yet?"

I looked into the pitiful face of my captor. His dark brown hair was long and shaggy and fell over his forehead. His eyebrows were narrowed and his pitiful blue eyes glared at me with brown bags underneath. He had a scruffy beard like he hadn't shaved in months. His cheeks were sunken and his skin was pale. I didn't recognize him. I gritted my teeth. Revenge was going to be so sweet I thought before answering.

"No, should I?"

"Look a little closer. Cast your mind back five years. When you were still just Charlie Parker, a nobody trying to make it big."

I was pissed off now. Who the fuck was this little jumped up shit who thought he could kidnap me? I was Charlie Parker and yeah I had money and lots of it, but that wasn't a reason for this. I tried to think back five years. Had I wronged someone. He didn't look to be any older than me and I didn't remember anything major from that time.

"Nope, can't say I remember you."

I knew I was getting to him. The smile vanished from his face and he was pacing back and forth, clenching his fists. His dark brown boots kicked at the floor and although his leather jacket was supposed to make him appear menacing, I found myself laughing.

"Find this amusing do you Charlie boy?"

He turned and anger flashed in his eyes as he pulled a knife from his jacket.

"Let's see how pretty that smile is when it spreads from ear to ear, shall we?

He held the knife at the corner of my mouth adding just enough pressure so that it pierced my skin.

"What do you want?" I asked tilting my head back away from the blade.

"Revenge, I want revenge. You took everything from me and I'm gonna make you pay. You think you're untouchable in your big penthouse with all your money and luxury, but I know you. I know your kind and when I'm finished you'll know what it's like to lose everything."

His nose almost touched mine as he spoke, spit sprayed my face as he raged.

"You're going to pay Charlie boy, and I'm going to be the one to make it happen."

He was fucking nuts, a psycho. I needed to keep him talking so that I could find out more. The more he talked, the more I could plan my escape.

"So we know each other then and I obviously wronged you somehow?"

He was pacing again but turned suddenly. His eyes were dancing.

"You took everything from me…. everything."

He combed his fingers through his lank brown hair, lifting it away from his forehead, deep in thought. If I had to guess, I'd say he was remembering this so called wrong I had inflicted on him five years ago. I thought back. At that time, I was just starting my company, just beginning to make something of myself. I still couldn't place this guy though. Something about the way he kept pulling his hair seemed familiar, like a memory itching at the back of my brain but it wouldn't come. I tried wriggling my hands again to loosen the ropes while I watched him pace. He was still holding the knife, a threat that I could do nothing about. My hands were bound tight but with the blood seeping into the rope I might just be able to get them free if I kept trying.

"So, where are we?" I asked.

He turned and smirked. "Someplace no one will ever find you, and even if they do, by the time they get here you'll be nothing but a rotting corpse."

"So you're planning to kill me then?"

I had to keep him talking, convince him that I wasn't afraid. I knew Liz, she'd have the police looking for me. Thoughts of Liz filled my mind and I couldn't help but smile. I recalled our wedding vows, dancing on the yacht, and......oh shit, the small explosion in the engine room that caused the yacht to sink, Liz was.... she was okay, I vaguely remembered the water and swimming, but she was alive, we made it to the beach. I know we did. I remembered her crying and then nothing. I had to get this son of a bitch to talk, to tell me what he'd done to her. If he'd harmed her in any way, I swear he'd pay.

"Oh yes, you're going to die alright but not until I've destroyed you, taken everything from you. You're going to regret ever interfering in my life."

He was still pacing and I could see that his body was trembling. His grip on the knife wouldn't hold if it kept up. My mind was reeling and I still had no fucking idea who he was.

"Look, mate, I really have no idea who you are. Perhaps if you tell me we can work this out."

I was trying to be diplomatic, use my business dealing

skills. It didn't work. He turned, the look in his eyes told me he was definitely unstable.

"You don't know me huh, well believe me Charlie boy, by the time I'm finished with you, my name will be the last thing you ever fucking forget. You think you're so smart, so fucking clever, but I knew, I knew you had her and I waited and waited till you let her go. You think you did good, but you, you Charlie fucking hot shot, you fucking killed her. It was all your fault," he said waving his hands in the air.

He was definitely losing it now. I'd never killed anyone.

"Who, who did I fucking kill?" I shouted at him. He was pissing me off now, tying me up, thinking he could keep me captive. He was wrong when he'd said I'd pay, very wrong because when this shit was over it would be my name that he'd scream with his last breath.

I pulled hard against the ropes on my wrist, searching the floor for anything I could grab with my feet. It was a mistake. I only took my eyes off him for a second but in that time, he was on me. His hand gripped my throat as he leaned into my face, snarling like a crazed lunatic.

"Susan," he spat at me. "You fucking killed Susan."

He let go shaking his head. His body was trembling with rage.

"Who the fuck is Susan?" I shouted.

With that, he lashed out. The knife he gripped tightly sliced down the side of my face tearing my skin open. I felt the blood trickle down my cheek as I jerked my head back away from him.

"Don't you speak her name," he screamed as he began pacing and mumbling to himself.

Susan, the name rattled around in my head. Susan, five years ago. These were my only clues as I wracked my brains trying to come up with what I had done. Five years ago, I'd just bought my apartment. I thought back to that time and then it hit me. Susan, the girl who'd broken in, the thief I'd caught. She'd been trying to break into the safe when I'd caught her and she'd put up one hell of a fight. I locked her in one of the rooms while I decided what to do. Man, she kicked and screamed for hours before she went quiet. It was the silence that got to me in the end and I went into the room to make sure she was okay. She was splayed out and barely breathing. As I moved closer to her I noticed the needle marks in her arms. She'd been high and now she was just out of it. There was something about her fragile state that spoke to me, made me want to help her. And I did. I didn't call the police and have her carted away. Instead, I sat with her, trying to offer some comfort as I waited for help to arrive. I remembered how she mumbled different names over and over again while I sat and reassured her that she would be fine. She spat in my face and was so full of anger when my mom's friend came to take her away. I'd had no choice. I had no idea how to deal with a drug addict, but I knew my mother had connections and she wouldn't ask any questions. We organized a private rehabilitation center for her and I visited a number of times over the next couple of weeks as she detoxed and got clean. On my last visit, she thanked me for saving her life. How could I have forgotten her?

I shook my head, breaking free from the memories as I watched my crazed kidnapper pace back and forth, muttering to himself. His shakes were getting worse.

"I didn't lay a finger on her, you're Susan. All I did was help her." I said aloud.

On hearing my words, he turned again, the rage in his eyes so noticeable.

"You took her from me and now you will pay. You will pay with your life and the lives of all those who mean something to you. You think you helped her, you didn't. You're the one who killed her."

He was screaming at me now, the knife swinging through the air as he waved his arms about. I had to get him to calm down or I wasn't going to last much longer. The ropes that bound my wrists were too tight and my efforts to loosen them had failed. My body was tired and I could feel myself slipping. I needed to stay awake, stay focused until help arrived. I swallowed hard. I was so thirsty. How long had I been without water and what was the likelihood of getting any from this lunatic? He'd stopped pacing now and my senses were on high alert. I'd seen this before, addicts coming down off a high were so unpredictable. One wrong word and I was toast. I should have seen it earlier, should have noticed, but my thoughts were on Liz and escape. He was on the edge right now and he needed another fix and soon. Did he have it with him? Was he gonna have to leave? If he did leave it could give me a chance to plan my escape and call for help.

"There is no escape for you Charlie boy, none. I will decide when your time is up you hear?"

He must have seen me looking around. He was clever I'd give him that, but he was still going to need his fix and while he was high and oblivious to me, I would make my move. My throat was beginning to close and I was struggling to even make enough spit to swallow.

"I need water" I coughed.

"Do you now," he glared.

He seemed to stop and think before moving to the furthest corner of the room. I couldn't see him now but I heard a tap run. I licked my dry lips in anticipation. He walked slowly back towards me, the cup in his hand trembling. Drops of water were spilling on the dusty floor. I licked my lips again and he smirked.

"You really want it don't you Charlie boy? Well here you go" he said throwing the cup of water in my face. The water splashed all over me and my tongue lashed out trying to capture as much as I could, licking the remains that trailed down to my chin.

"I ain't giving you nothing, I'm gonna enjoy watching you beg for your life."

"You sick son of a bitch, you'll pay for this," I snapped.

It was a very foolish move but I couldn't help myself. I wasn't putting up with this anymore. I pulled on the ropes feeling them shred my skin but I didn't care, I'd had enough of this shit now. He was going to pay. I rattled my wrists back and forth, pulling with all my strength. It was no fucking use; the ropes weren't giving an inch.

All the while he stood staring, smirking at me and I could feel my blood boil.

*Oh, when I get out of here he'd pay. He'd curse the day he ever heard the name, Charlie Parker.*

I slumped back against the post I was tied to. Defeated and exhausted.

"Finished now?"

I looked away from him in disgust. All I wanted to do was pound his face till there was nothing left of it and he knew it.

"Tut, tut, Charlie boy, tantrums won't get you anywhere. I have a special treat for you."

I turned my gaze towards him. He was holding a syringe coming closer to me.

"It's a little present just for you Charlie boy, let's see if your body likes it, shall we?"

"Get the fuck away from me," I shouted kicking out with my feet.

"Now, now, you'll only feel a little prick, and then I promise you'll feel so much better."

He was getting closer now and there was nothing I could do. I thrashed as much as I could until he held the knife to my throat.

"Keep it up and I'll slice you from ear to ear."

I stilled. I had no choice. I had to survive this for Liz. I had to get out of here and find her. She was my world and I had promised her, till death do us part. That wasn't going to be today. I felt the sting of the needle and the cold fluid entering my arm. I felt it seep into my system slowly clouding my mind as darkness took over.

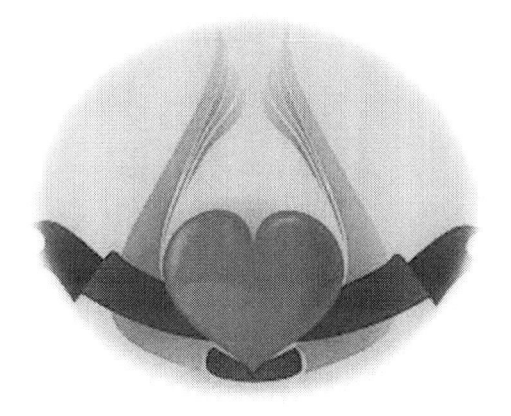

# LIZ

It took a little over an hour before the island came into sight. I'd spent that time thinking about Charles. How we'd met, how he'd helped me to feel again after losing my parents, and how I'd fallen hopelessly in love with him. He'd pulled me from rock bottom and without him I'm sure I wouldn't be alive today. I didn't tell John this little detail, how my mind had fractured, how I'd lost my will to live after my parents were mowed down by a drunk driver. I needed him to believe I was sane if I was ever going to get to the island. I'd explained as much as I could remember about the explosion on the yacht. My memories were still a little hazy, but at least I knew it was from the drugs that had been found in my system. I still had no clue how they got there but that didn't matter. Once I found Charles he would take care of everything. He would fix things and I'd be safe again.

The island was getting closer now and I could just about make out the beach.

"I'm almost there Charles," I whispered into the sea air. "We'll be together soon."

"We'll anchor here," John said pulling me from my memories. "We'll take the small boat, water's too shallow to take this girl any further."

"Okay," I mumbled, my eyes firmly fixed on the beach.

"Come on then,"

I stood and moved to the side where John was untying ropes.

"You jump in and I'll lower the boat down."

"Huh," I said looking confused.

"The small boat, it's just over the edge, you hop in first and I'll lower us down."

I nodded and climbed into the small boat. John followed and lowered us down into the calm waters before grabbing the oars. His strong arms moved back and forth as our small boat headed in the direction of the island, and Charles.

As it got nearer time seemed to slow, seconds passing like minutes, minutes like hours until I saw it. Flocks of seagulls circling and diving to the sand, pulling and tugging.

*Oh my god Charles, they're eating Charles.*

I didn't give it a second thought before I plunged into the sea. My mind was focused only on getting to him, rescuing him. I needed Charles. I was nothing without him. Swimming as fast as I could I buried the images of what those seagulls were doing in the back of my mind.

"Liz, what the hell are you doing?" I heard John shout from the boat.

I ignored him focused only on getting to that beach, to

my Charles. I stood as soon as I could, and ran through the shallow waves with my hands above my head, screaming and shouting at the birds circling Charles' body. It was still there, exactly as I left it.

"Oh Charles," I sobbed as I fell to my knees in front of him.

I couldn't bring myself to look at the damage those birds would have inflicted. I buried my head in my hands and let the tears flow.

"I'm so sorry I left you. I'm so sorry...."

"Liz."

I heard John but my mind just wouldn't compute. I was lost in a sea of grief.

"Liz, look at me."

I raised my head, his tone was so soft I couldn't help myself.

"It's not him Liz, look."

I lowered my eyes taking in Charles' black slacks covering his long legs, moving up to the white shirt that covered his muscular chest. It was still covered in his blood. I swallowed deeply before bringing my eyes to his face. I stared in silence. It wasn't my Charles. This was something else. There were tears in the skin, but no blood. What was it?

"What is it?" I asked looking up at John.

He nodded his head, his hand placed across his nose. I hadn't even noticed the smell but it wafted through my nostrils now and I felt my stomach heave. It was the same smell I remembered. The smell of death.

"It's a dummy, Liz. It's not Charles," he said moving closer and dropping to his knees to get a closer look.

"Someone did a pretty good job of setting this up. That stench, that's rotten blood. The dummy is covered in it." He said lifting the arms and letting them drop, before inspecting the tears in the dummy's face.

My body was in shock. I didn't know what to think. It looked like Charles. It was dressed like Charles, but I could see now that it wasn't him. My hands were shaking as I reached out to touch whatever it was that was in front of me. I hesitated as my hand got closer. My fingertips brushed off the body and it felt cold, but not flesh cold if that makes sense. It felt like rubber. I gripped the arm harder, it squashed in my hand. There were no bones. John was right, it was a dummy. I felt bile rising and turned my head emptying the contents of my stomach onto the sand. Feeling better I took in a deep breath.

"It's not him," I whispered. "It's not my Charles."

I looked once more at the body in front of me. How could I have been so stupid? How did I not know? My tears flowed as I grasped the reality of what was happening.

"What have I done?"

John placed a hand on my shoulder. "It's not your fault Liz, you couldn't have known, you'd been drugged remember. This was staged, you were meant to think it was Charles. Someone went to a lot of trouble to set this up."

"But Charles was here, he was, we both were and he was hurt, his breathing." I paused taking a deep breath before I continued. "His breathing was bad and I passed out," I sobbed.

I needed to get the words out. I needed to say them.

"When I woke his breathing had stopped. He was cold."

I lost control then and guilt consumed me.

"What did I do? It's all my fault. I fell asleep. It was Me."

"Liz, this is not your fault do you hear me?"

I'd never heard John use such a harsh tone. It shocked me

and I looked up at him.

"It wasn't your fault," he said a little softer. "Come on, get up. He's not here. We need to get back to the ship."

I looked down at the pretend body and shook my head.

"I can't. Charles is here somewhere and I'm going to find him. I'm not leaving John. I'm not."

An unknown strength had taken over me. I had failed Charles when I passed out. I wouldn't fail him again. He was here somewhere and I was going to find him. I was going to bring him home and give him the proper burial he deserved.

"Let's get back to the ship. We can think about what to do next when we get there."

"I'm not leaving John. Charles was here and I'm going to find him."

"Liz, you need to think. You need time to process all of this."

"Stop," I shouted. "I'm not leaving here. You go if you want to, but my Charles is here somewhere and I'm going to find him."

I was losing it. My body was shaking, with what, I don't know, fear, pain, adrenaline, or maybe it was hope. It wasn't Charles' body so maybe he was still alive and he could be hurt. I jumped to my feet, a surge of energy flowing through me.

"What if he's still alive John? What if he's hurt? I have to look; I have to be sure."

John looked worried. I could tell he didn't believe me. He thought I was crazy. I knew that look, I'd seen it before after my parents died. The doctors looked at me like that.

"Don't look at me like that, I'm not crazy," I shouted.

John's face paled. "I'm sorry Liz. This is all just too familiar for me. Susan, she...."

"I'm not Susan and I'm not crazy," I said cutting him off.

"Now you can help me or go home. The choice is yours."

I don't know where the strength came from but I started to walk towards the trees. I remembered them. I'd hidden behind them when the so-called pirates had arrived on the beach.

"Wait, Liz, you've no idea where you're going," John said running to catch up with me. "We don't know this island," he said putting his hand on my shoulder to stop me.

I turned and looked at him. My tears were rolling down my cheeks again.

"I know," I sobbed. "But I have to do something, I can't just leave."

John looked at me, really looked at me. "Fine, but I think we need to contact the authorities. They need to know what is going on. I'll help you search for Charles, but only if you let me call for backup."

I nodded giving my permission as I tried to come up with a plan. Charles had been injured. I knew that much. His shirt had been stained with blood. Even if he did manage to move away from me, he wouldn't have gotten far.

While I waited for John to finish the call he was making to the police, another thought that filled me with dread took control. What if Charles had meant to leave me? What if this was planned and he left me here to die?

*Don't be silly, Charles loves you. He'd never leave you.*

So, did my parents I thought. They loved me, said they'd never leave and they did. They left me alone with no one. They chose to abandon me because I'm not worth it. I'm broken and I can't be fixed. Only Charles could fix me and maybe he got sick of me too. My constant need for approval, my fear of him leaving. Maybe he sank the boat on purpose and drugged me. Maybe he did leave me here to die.

I sank to my knees, the soft sand cushioning my fall. I was sobbing uncontrollably.

"It'll be fine Liz. Don't you worry," John said sinking to his knees beside me.

He pulled me into his chest and cradled my head on his shoulder as I let the tears flow.

"What if Charles did all this? What if he left me here to die?" I whispered.

"Shush, don't think like that. We'll find him, you wait and see."

I didn't know what I'd done to deserve John, but at that moment I knew I would be lost without him. He was the strength I needed to carry on.

Once my tears stopped and I managed to get control of myself I looked up at John.

"What do we do?" I asked.

"Well, I've been thinking. No one's been here since the men the other day and they didn't get the chance to explore or look around because you went a little psycho on them," he grinned. "There could be some clues here that might tell us what happened to Charles."

"I didn't move around or explore either," I said. "The furthest I went was to the trees and that was to hide from the others."

"Didn't pan out too well, though," John smirked and for the first time in days, I felt a smile creep across my face.

"Come on, let's make a start. The police should be here in a couple of hours, maybe by then we'll have more information to give them."

I stared up at this man who was willing to help me.

"What are we looking for?"

I felt useless. I had no idea what to do. I'd never done

anything. I'd always been told what to do, how to behave. My father even told me what to study in school. I didn't know how to make a decision on my own. I'd even let Charles' mother make all the wedding arrangements. Even the thought of trying to figure things out had me in a panic. How was I going to be of help? What could I possibly do to help find Charles?

"Come on. We'll start from the trees," John said pulling me from my pity parade. "There could be tracks or something we can follow. It's not a very big island you know?"

"It's not?" I said feeling a shred of hope building.

He smiled. "Where were you supposed to be staying anyway?"

"I don't know," I frowned. "Charles planned everything, but he said the house was amazing and that I'd love it."

"Right, well that's our starting point so. We'll head to the trees look for any sign of footprints and then go find this house. It could hold the answers you've been looking for."

I heard something in his voice when he mentioned the house. Was there even a house? Was he thinking that Charles had brought me here to murder me? It didn't make any sense. I had nothing so killing me didn't achieve anything unless Charles was just tired of me and knew I wouldn't live without him. Maybe getting rid of me was the only way he could be free? My mind was really messing with my thoughts now. Shaking them off I followed John as he headed towards the trees. I needed to remain positive. Charles was out here and he was hurt and I was going to find him.

We stopped once we reached the trees.

"How were you meant to get to your house on this island anyway?" John asked.

"I don't know. Charles said we wouldn't have far to walk once we docked so it can't be too far from here."

"Hmmm, but the yacht sank so we don't know where you were supposed to dock. It's a good job the island isn't that big. It shouldn't take us too long to find it."

I nodded in agreement as I remembered the last time I crouched behind these trees. I was convinced my world had ended. We moved through the thin lining of trees and my breath stopped.

"Wow."

John paused, "beautiful, isn't it?"

"Yes"

It was all I could manage to get out. We were standing on the top of a hill looking down at the rest of the island. It was stunning. There was a harbor and a couple of houses scattered here and there as well as a long white sandy beach that stretched along the coastline.

"Charles said our house was on the beach," I said scanning the rooftops that were visible.

"That narrows things down. There're only two properties on the beach," John said motioning to a root top to his left. "There's that one to your left and another just past the harbor. Which one do you think it is Liz?"

"I don't know," I said looking at both. I tried to recall everything Charles had said to me.

"You'll love it, Liz, you can walk straight from the bed to the beach," Charles grinned. I could feel his excitement.

"Won't people see us?"

"No, our house is totally private, there're no other properties around. We'll have to take the jeep if we want to go anywhere. Mind you, the island isn't that big and I've made sure everything we need is in the house," he said wiggling his eyebrows at me. "You see, Mrs. Parker, there really is no need for us to leave the bedroom until it's time to go home."

I laughed and slapped his shoulder. He was such a tease.

"Liz, which property?" John asked bringing me back to reality.

"That one," I said point at the lone house to the left. "Charles said there were no other houses near us."

"Well then, let's get moving. You keep your eyes peeled for anything suspicious you hear, we've no idea what happened to you or why and the police won't get here for a good while yet."

I swallowed hard. I really didn't want to think about that now. What I wanted was to imagine Charles sitting waiting for me inside our honeymoon house. Taking one last look at the property in the distance, I put my head down and started following John towards whatever lay in wait. It didn't look that far and the trees were easy enough to get through. It wasn't a dense forest or anything, just enough cover to ensure privacy.

As we reached the beach house all was quiet. There was no indication that anyone was here or had been in the past couple of days. It was quiet, too quiet, and John motioned for me to stop as he looked around.

"Stay here while I check things out."

I stood in the safety of the palm trees as I watched him move from window to window. The beach house was impressive. Two stories high with a porch wrapping around the exterior. The outside was wrapped in wood cladding that blended neatly into the surroundings. John disappeared around the back of the house and I waited taking in the view. Such perfection. Two weeks here would be bliss. No distractions, the beach outside my door and the soft whisper of the waves ebbing and flowing onto the pure white sand. It was the honeymoon destination dreams were made of, although in my case this would be remembered as a nightmare. John appeared from the other side of the house.

"All clear," he beckoned. "No one's home."

I moved from the tree line and made my way towards the house that should have been my home. It felt strange to be here without Charles. I could just imagine him carrying me over the threshold, laughing and joking. I brushed a tear from my eye and chastised myself.

*Pull it together, you need to get through this.*

I followed John around the back of the property. The entire back of the house was made up of glass windows from floor to ceiling with a balcony opening onto the beach. It was stunning.

"The door's unlocked," John said. "I think we should look around, there might be something in here that will help."

John nudged the door open, his watchful eyes taking everything in. I followed amazed as I took in the expansive kitchen. It was pristine. Black granite counter tops set against white gloss presses. The smell of flowers filled the air. Lilies my favorite, Charles did this for me. I walked through into the hallway checking for any signs that Charles had been here. Pausing at the teak staircase I looked up. Panic and anxiety seeped into my body as I made my way step by step.

*Please don't let me find a body, please don't let me find his body.*

I repeated the mantra till I reached the top. There were three doors to the left and another three to the right. I chose the door in front of me and pushed it open. My hand flew to my mouth as I gasped in awe. It was the master bedroom. A huge bed filled the space decorated with crisp white linen. With tears in my eyes, I stepped across the threshold as my nose was assaulted with the smell of roses. The bed was covered in little red and white petals. I couldn't hold back the sobs that escaped as my hand clasped firmly over my mouth. I moved forward and ran my fingers through the petals that were starting to wilt. He did all this for me. I paused that the top of the bed. There was a small box sitting on the pillow to the left. The side I always slept on. I reached for it, cradling it in my hands before slowly lifting the lid. Tears fell from my eyes as I tried to focus on the delicate necklace that lay inside. A silver heart, nothing intricate, just a plain heart with a small ruby in the middle. I picked it up and smiled. He does know me so well. I turned the heart over and found an inscription that said together for eternity and both our names engraved in delicate font. I placed the box against my heart and made a promise to myself that I would find Charles no matter what.

The sound of John's heavy footsteps coming up the stairs made me turn.

"There's plenty of food, you hungry?" He said taking in the tears streaming down my face.

I shrugged and made my way towards him.

"He planned everything so perfectly," I said. "I have to find him, John."

"We will, but come on let's grab a bite to eat and get going. There must be some clues as to what happened. The cops will be here soon and once that happens they won't let us near the place."

I nodded in agreement and we made our way to the kitchen. John had laid out two plates of salad along with some cold cuts and we tucked in, eating in silence.

"You done?" John asked standing to clear the plates.

I nodded, I hadn't realized how hungry I was until I started eating.

"What now?" I asked.

"Well, I was thinking. Charles's body was taken from the beach so there must be clues somewhere and whoever took him had to have a plan. They knew you'd be here so they had to have had somewhere to stay here on the island. Down by the harbor is too busy so my guess is that there is another place nearby."

I listened. John had given this a lot of thought and he knew what he was talking about.

"I'm thinking we search around this property and look for anything that's out of place. If we can't find anything we head back to the beach and wait for the cops," He continued.

"Okay, so what exactly are we looking for?" I asked.

"You said Charles was injured so that means whoever took him had to be very strong if they carried him, or they had some sort of transport. Any tracks on the beach would be long gone now but up the hill, they'd still be visible and down here where there's very little traffic. I say we start outside and see what we can find."

"You believe me now?" I asked. "You believe Charles is real and that he was with me on the beach?"

"I do, I believe you, but I also think there's a lot more to this than we know."

"But what if he left me on that beach, what if he just wanted to be rid of me?"

"Look around Liz, the petals on the bed, the necklace, does that seem like someone who wanted to get rid of you?"

"No," I said realizing how silly I was being.

Leaving the beach house behind, we began our search. John took the left side of the property while I made my way to the right. The ground was dry and dusty with white sand sprinkled all over. I walked slowly, my eyes focused on the ground, looking for anything that might seem out of place.

"Anything?" John shouted from behind.

I looked up in dismay. "Nothing," I said.

"Okay, well I think we should keep going left. It's a bit more secluded this way and my bet is if you were planning on taking someone you wouldn't want to be in plain sight. The trees offer great coverage."

I followed, my hope fading. I was beginning to lose faith. Charles had just vanished. I thought back to the petals on our bed and smiled. He didn't leave me. He was taken. That thought alone brought me some comfort and I picked up my pace and caught up with John. There was a pathway through the trees on the other side of the beach house and I knew Charles and I would have walked this trek hand in hand with a picnic. My eyes began to water again as I thought of all the amazing things we could be doing. Instead I was alone with a man I'd only met, trying to find his body.

"Look, over here, I've found blood," John stopped pointing at the ground.

"Is it Charles?"

"Now, I can't tell that Liz, but it is something. Let's keep going. We're on the right track."

As I reached his side my eyes found the blood that had stained the sand red. It wasn't a lot just a few drops and I was grateful for that. My heart raced. We were on the right track.

*I'm coming, Charles. I'm coming. Don't give up.*

With renewed hope, we continued through the trees. We followed the pathway till it opened into a small clearing. The scenery was breathtaking. We could see for miles. The cool clear Ocean and white sandy beaches stretched out in front of us. I could see yachts bobbing up and down on the water in the distance and the smell of the salt air caused me to lift my head to the sky. We stopped for a moment as John looked around for more clues.

"I don't see anything. Let's keep going."

We walked through the clearing towards the palm trees that lined the perimeter taking us back down the hill to the other side of the island. The ground was more uneven now and I had to hold onto the trees to keep my balance at times. We hadn't gotten very far when John held his hand up motioning for me to stop. He turned with his finger to his lips signaling that I be quiet. I moved towards him taking in what he was looking at. It was a wooden shack, nothing special. It looked dark and deserted. There was no car, no sign of life, just a rusty wheelbarrow and a shovel sitting outside the door.

"Wait here behind the trees while I look and keep out of sight."

I was glad I didn't have to go down there. I crept behind the trees and watched as John made his way down. The dingy cabin didn't look like much. There was one dirty window and a door, that's all I could see. It was probably a hunting cabin or a place to shelter from the rain if the island ever had rain. I really had no idea. I knew nothing about this island except for the fact that I was to spend two blissful weeks here with Charles on our honeymoon. I sniffled. Every time I thought of Charles the tears would come. I knew I shouldn't let them. I knew I had to be strong, but who was I kidding. I couldn't do anything without him. It was Charles that kept me alive. Without him I was nothing. I wiped away the tears. I couldn't see John. He'd gone around the back of the cabin. I watched in anticipation, waiting for him to signal that it was okay.

Without warning the cabin door opened and a man stepped out. He was tall, disheveled with dark hair that flopped in front of his eyes. He raised a hand and pushed it back. I watched as he leaned forward and picked up the shovel. I gasped and ducked behind the tree.

*What do I do? What do I do? Oh, God someone please help.*

I was shaking. I didn't know what to do. Should I shout, warn John? I couldn't get my brain to think straight.

*Get a grip Liz. Just shut up and keep still. John will be fine.*

I bit my lip as I watched the shovel rise into the air just before John came around from the back of the house. He didn't see him. He had no idea what was going to happen. I went to shout to warn him but my body froze as the shovel came down across the top of his head and knocked him to the ground. I stared in horror as the man reached down and dragged John by the feet into the cabin.

*Oh, my God, what am I going to do now? John's gone, dead. I'm on my own.*

My stomach lurched as I bent over and the food we'd had for lunch spilled out onto the ground. My body was trembling. I leaned back against the tree. What was I going to do now? My mind was a useless mess of fear. I was going to die out here. I'd be next and there was nothing I could do. I pulled at my hair in frustration.

Get a grip Liz. You're his only chance now. You need to figure out a way to get him out of there. My inner voice screamed at me.

*I can't, what if there's more than one man in there? What can I do? I'm nothing.*

That's the old you talking Liz. You are someone now remember. You are Charles' someone and he needs you, so does John. My inner self always had a way of rationalizing things. People thought I was crazy talking to myself but it was how I worked things out. How I calmed myself when I started falling apart.

I took a deep breath and turned back towards the beach house. If I was going to rescue John, I needed to come up with a plan. The police would be here soon too.

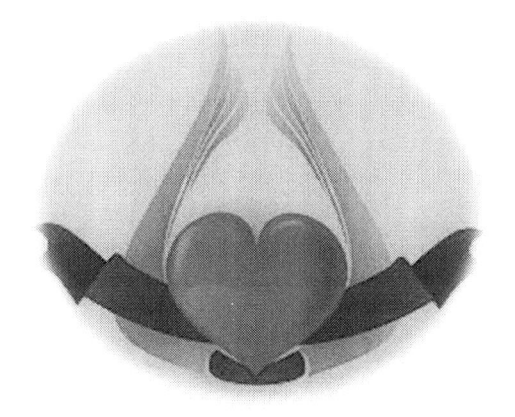

# **CHARLES**

A dragging sound woke me from my drug induced slumber. I pried my eyes open, the throbbing pain in my head reminding me of the torture I had faced. My vision slowly came into focus and I saw my captor dragging a body through the door of the cabin. I had no idea who it was, another victim no doubt of his crazed revenge. The body was dumped beside me. I couldn't tell whether he was still alive.

"Looks like you have a bit of company Charlie boy. Do you recognize him?"

I looked at the man and shook my head. I had no idea who he was.

"Not one of yours then huh?"

"I've never seen him before," I said studying the face of the insane lunatic that stood before me.

"Not to worry," he said going back to close the door. "Glad to see you're awake, though. Time for phase two of my plan. It's a good one Charlie, you just wait and see."

He was grinning away to himself as I struggled to move. My hands were still bound tightly. I heard a wheeze from beside me and knew that whoever this poor guy was he was still breathing.

"Who is he?" I asked.

"No idea, caught him snooping around outside. Seems to be on his own, but I'm going out to check. You play nicely while I'm gone you hear me?"

I watched him pick up a gun off the table as he made his way through the door.

"Fuck, I didn't see the gun," I whispered.

A knife was bad enough but now he had a gun too. I had to get out of here and fast.

"Hey, hey you," I said as I leaned towards the man beside me. He didn't move. "Hey," I repeated, louder this time.

His body twitched and he started to stir. His hand immediately went to the back of his head as he opened his eyes.

"You okay?" I asked.

He shook his head, probably trying to focus before he turned to me.

"Charles?" he stuttered.

"Yeah. How do you know my name? Who are you?"

"The name's John. I'm here with Liz. Who the hell is that guy?"

Liz. He said, Liz. She was okay. My Liz was okay, that bastard hadn't killed her. I let out a deep breath and then the horror hit me. That fucking lunatic was gone out there with a gun.

"Where is she? Is she okay?"

It was all I could manage as terror gripped my body.

"Yeah, she's fine. I told her to stay hidden. The cops are on their way man, but I don't know when they'll arrive. Who is that guy?"

I swallowed deeply. Liz was safe. She wasn't stupid. She'd follow the rules. She'd hide. I knew she would. Liz always did what anyone told her to do. It was one of the things that pissed me off. She was a people pleaser, always looking for approval. I hated it and was working so hard on building her confidence. I don't know what went on with her and her parents but whatever it was, they'd broken, my girl.

John cleared his throat and I realized that I hadn't answered his question.

"I've no idea who this lunatic is, but I'm telling you he's unstable. We've got to get out of here. Can you untie me? He could be back any second."

John sat up, wobbling. That blow to the head must have been something. He scooted over beside me and began loosening my binds. The relief was instant. Rubbing the deep welts that were now visible I stood for the first time in days. Looking down at where John sat, I paused.

"Where are we?" I asked

"Still on the island, not far from your beach house."

That's good, I thought. At least I know where I am. A noise from outside alerted me to the fact that my captor had returned. I sat back against the wooden pole I'd been tied to and resumed my position. John quickly retied my hands, loose enough that I could escape when needed.

"Don't move till I give the word," I whispered. "You're still dizzy and I'm too weak to jump him just yet."

There was no point in trying to rush this guy when he

came through the door. John couldn't stand and I was too weak to do much. I nodded to John as he resumed his position. If we had any chance of escaping, we needed to take him by surprise. With renewed hope, I smiled to myself knowing that revenge would soon be mine.

"No sign of our friend waking up then Charlie boy?" my captor said as he came through the door and looked in our direction. "Not a problem, it's you I want anyway," he sneered as he walked in our direction.

He stopped in front of John looking down at his crumpled body before kicking him in the legs.

"So you ready for phase two then?"

I glared at him trying to restrain myself. I wanted so much to jump up and kick the shit out of him, beat him to a pulp. I knew there was no point, though, not until I found out what he had planned. He was still holding a bloody gun too. A knife wound I could take, a bullet was a different story.

"Do your worst," I spat out.

He rolled his head and laughed.

"Oh Charlie boy, you're gonna love this. For my next little trick, I'm gonna make your parents disappear."

What the fuck. My eyes shot to his face.

"Ha, now I have your attention, don't I? You wanna save your parents, then you are going to sign your company and everything you own over to me."

I clenched my teeth. "Never," I roared. I knew I wouldn't be able to keep still for much longer. "You touch my parents and I'll...."

He cut me off. "You'll what Charlie boy? There's nothing you can do to me. You think I care about death threats? You took everything from me remember? Now it's my turn to return the favor. You're going to regret ever setting eyes on my

Susan."

His Susan. This guy was clearly deranged. I didn't take her. All I did was help her beat her drug habit.

"I never took her from you," I shouted. "All I did was help the poor girl kick her drug habit."

I felt the gun against my temple.

"She was mine," he spat. "You had no right. Thought you helped her, did you? Well, you didn't. It's your fault she's dead and now you'll pay. Your parents are about to meet their maker if you don't sign everything over to me."

"Okay, okay," I shouted. I needed to keep him stable just a little longer. Once that gun was out of his hands we'd jump him. I wasn't taking a bullet now that I knew Liz was okay and I couldn't put John's life at risk either. I just had to hold it together for another few minutes.

"That's right Charlie boy, I hold the power here," he said waving the gun. "Your tough guy act won't help you. If you don't sign the papers your parents are dead."

"You touch my parents and I swear you'll pay," I seethed.

There was no way he could harm my parents. They were in the Bahamas. Liz and I were to meet up with them for a couple of days before heading home.

"Think I'm bluffing, do you?" He sneered before turning to walk towards the table. He put the gun down and picked up some papers and a phone. He tapped and swiped a few times before walking back with a sick grin on his face.

"I never lie," he said as he shoved the phone in my face.

My entire body went cold as I looked at my mom and dad bound and gagged. The fear in their eyes would stay with me forever.

"You sick bastard," I shouted. "If anything happens to them I'll…"

"You'll what Charlie boy, you'll kill me," he laughed. "It won't make any difference, if I don't make a call in 20 minutes they're toast, and once again you'll be responsible for someone else's death."

I grimaced. What the fuck was I going to do now? The gun was gone but jumping him now wasn't going to do any good. I had to make sure my parents were safe first.

"Okay, okay," I said. "I'll sign the goddam papers, just make your fucking call."

"Wise decision Charlie boy," he sneered. "Pity you couldn't have done that five years ago. None of this would be happening if you had. You think you're the big tough CEO. Well, let me tell you something. You're nothing and by the time I've finished with you, you'll know it. I'm going to take everything do you hear, and when I'm finished you'll know what real despair is. You'll know what it's like to have your whole life ripped away from you. I promise."

He turned and walked back to the table muttering away to himself. I looked down at John. His eyes were open and I mouthed to him to stay still. Just a little longer, just till my parents were safe. He nodded his understanding. I turned back to my captor and watched as he picked up the phone. He paced back and forth in front of the table before he started talking.

"Hold tight, he's signing now. Five minutes and you're good to go. I'll text when it's done."

He ended the call and grinned. I had no idea what he meant or whether this lunatic would remain true to his word. All I knew was that I had to ensure my parents were safe. Picking up the stack of papers off the table he made his way back towards me.

"This is how it's gonna go Charlie boy. You're gonna sign

these papers and your parents will be allowed to live."

I glared at him, anger rising in my body. As soon as he bent to untie me I was going to unleash hell. He had no idea what was coming to him. I would put an end to him and his sick plans. No one was taking my family away, no one. He may be a cocky fucker now but just wait till I got my hands around his throat, then I'd show him. You don't mess with Charlie Parker, ever.

He must have sensed it because he started laughing.

"Don't get any silly ideas now. I ain't as dumb as I might look." He still had the gun and it was pointed at John's head. "Do we understand each other?"

"Yeah," I spat.

We still couldn't make our escape. I wasn't going to be held responsible for getting someone shot.

There was a loud bang outside and he turned. His grip tightened on his gun as he turned and made for the door. He turned back and laughed.

"Stay here, I'll be back."

With that, he pulled the door tightly behind him.

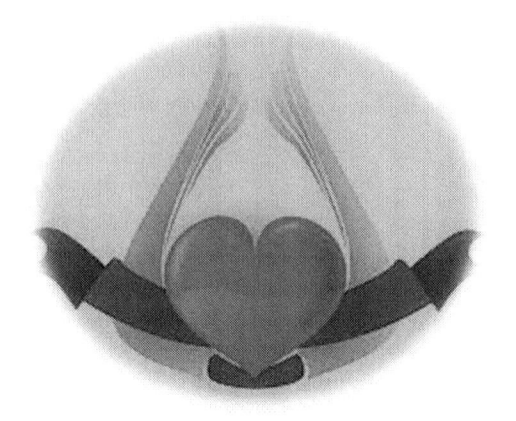

# LIZ

I watched frozen in terror as the man who'd attacked John appeared at the door of the cabin again. He was looking around, looking for me. He walked around the cabin his eyes searching. I knew I would have to move. If he walked towards me he'd see me. I crawled backward, watching him, making sure he didn't see me. When he went back around the cabin again I jumped up and ran. I didn't dare look back. I just ran, my heart thumping in my chest. When I reached the clearing I stopped. I couldn't run any further. My hands rested on my knees as I bent over gasping for air. What was I going to do now? John was gone? How was I going to find Charles? John said the police were coming but how long would they take? John could be dead and it was all my fault. I made him come with me to look for Charles. I put his life in danger. I should never have come here. I should have stayed on the beach and waited for the police. What was I thinking? I couldn't rescue Charles. I couldn't do anything on my own. I couldn't survive on my own. My father's voice drifted to my mind now and I knew he'd been right. He told me I could never do anything on my own. He told me that I needed him to survive, that I was worthless without him. He was right. I was worthless. What had I done since they died? Nothing. I was nothing. I'd curled up ready to die when they left. I knew I wouldn't make it on my own. I fell into darkness and it was only Charles that saw my light. He dragged me from the pit of despair that held me captive and helped me to live again. I never shared the horrors that I had endured with him. I never told him of the torment my father had placed in my mind. I wanted Charles to see me, to free me, and he did. I lived through him and now he was gone too. I couldn't be alone. I couldn't let the demons consume my mind again. I had to be strong. I had to fight.

*You can't be alone.*

My father's words went around and around in my mind. I knew they were right. I knew I couldn't do this. I would give anything right now to be back in the hospital. To have nurses and doctors looking after me. I would take the medication, feel the numbness it brought. I would be a good patient. I would. I was losing it. My mind was taking over and my father's words continued to taunt me. I took in a deep breath. Maybe I couldn't be alone. Maybe I was worthless, but for Charles, I could be strong. For Charles, I would do anything. I felt the little box in my pocket. Charles knew our love was eternal. What would he think if I gave up now?

*You need to be strong Liz. You need to do this for Charles.*

My inner voice was right. I needed to be strong right now. I needed to help John and find Charles. I took a deep breath and thought about what my next move should be. I could do exactly what John had done. I could sneak around the cabin, but unlike John, I would be prepared. I would be armed and waiting for that man when he came through the door. I'd be waiting and I'd bash him over the head with the shovel. I could rescue John and then together we'd find Charles. I felt a weight lift. I felt lighter now that I had a plan to follow.

I made my way back through the trees crouching low when I spotted the man from the cabin. He was shaking his head, giving up. I followed him back to the cabin. My eyes were peeled watching for any sudden movements. The shovel was outside the cabin. As I looked at it I realized that it was too heavy for me to lift and swing. I needed something smaller but strong at the same time. I spotted a small branch. That would do the trick. I grabbed it with both hands and made my way towards the cabin.

Now all you have to do is get him to come back outside.

My hands were shaking. My father's voice screaming inside my mind, but I refused to listen. I'd put John in danger and I needed to get him out of it. Gripping the branch as hard as I could I raised it over my head and brought it down with a bang against the side of the cabin. I raised it again as I waited for John's captor to step through the door. I was ready. I heard him muttering as I waited with my breath held and my hands trembling. As the door creaked open I swung the branch as hard as I could. I felt it connect and I watched as he fell to the ground. I turned and ran into the cabin. Stepping through the door I froze as my eyes met Charles'. He was alive. He was here.

"Charles," I said rushing towards him.

"Liz, what are you doing here? It's not safe," he said wrapping his arms around my waist, bringing his lips to my forehead.

I held him as hard as I could. He was alive. My Charles was here and he was alive. I was never letting go of him again. He stepped back, his arms still holding me.

"Are you okay, you're not hurt, are you?"

"I'm okay," I spluttered as the tears fell down my cheeks. I heard another sound and turned to see John standing, smiling at me.

"What did you do Liz? I told you to stay safe."

"Sorry John, I couldn't. I couldn't leave you here. I hit him over the head with a branch. He fell to the ground."

"We better get out of here and fast. He's got a gun," Charles said turning me back to him.

"Well, well, well. Looks like the little missus came to the rescue. You ready for some real fun now Charlie boy?"

I heard an evil laugh behind me and my heart stopped as I turned to face the monster that had caused me so much pain. He was just standing there, staring, a sneer on his face. He was exactly what I pictured evil to look like. Tall, skinny, rough looking. His hair was overgrown and dirty as it hung limply in his face. His eyes were dark and shadowed and he looked like he hadn't shaved in over a year, a scruffy beard covering his chin. His appearance sent shivers down my spine.

"Looks like I get to kill you all over again," he grinned.

I felt Charles stiffen.

"You fucking touch her and I'll kill you." Charles shouted.

"Now, now Charlie boy," the man said waving a gun in the air. "No need for such hostility. I told you, didn't I? I told you you'd feel despair, that I'd take everything from you and I will."

The gun was pointing at me now and everything moved

in slow motion as I watched his finger pull the trigger. A pain like nothing I'd ever felt before shot through my stomach and my hands gripped it as blood seeped out through them. I looked up at Charles, my head started to spin.

"No," I heard him scream as I fell forward into his arms. "Liz, you stay with me you hear. You can't leave me, just hold on."

I looked up into his eyes. My father was wrong. I wouldn't die alone.

"He was wrong," I whispered as I let the darkness take me.

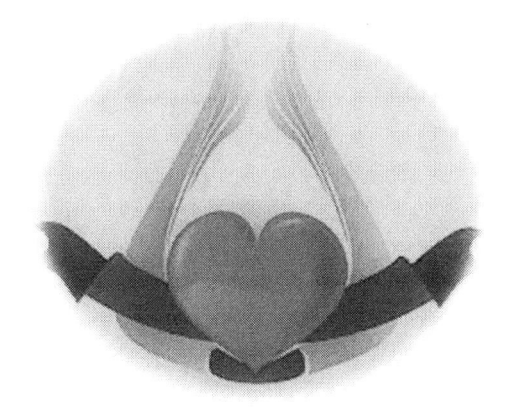

# CHARLES

One minute she was standing in front of me, my beautiful dark haired goddess, full of courage and fight, the next she staggered and fell forward into my arms her hands clutching her stomach as her blood seeped out through them. It was like being in a nightmare, the sound of the gunshot echoing in my ears over and over again. Her body felt so light in my arms, like she weighed nothing at all, as she looked up into my eyes. This couldn't be happening. I wouldn't let it happen. She stared at me as her body tensed.

"No," I screamed as her body went limp in my arms. "You can't leave me Liz, you have to fight, you have to stay strong, help is coming, just stay with me please."

I watched as she struggled with the pain. Her eyelids fluttering as she battled to keep them open. She couldn't die, not my Liz. She'd come too far. I tried to fight the tears but it was useless, I couldn't control the sobs that escaped me now and I didn't care. I looked up at the sick fuck in time to see John knock him to the ground. He was smiling, actually grinning as John punched him. His eyes met mine and he mouthed 'everything' at me, before John punched him again. He was right, I was about to lose everything. I would have given everything to trade places with Liz at that moment. She was my life, my everything, but I'd gladly die for her. I'd lived, I'd tasted success, and I knew what it meant to love with all my heart. Liz had just found life again. She couldn't lose it.

I placed my hand over hers and applied pressure, just like they do in the movies.

"Stay with me darling, just try to stay awake, help is on the way, it won't be long now I promise."

She looked up at me, such love in her eyes as she tried to smile. She opened her mouth to speak but I hushed her. "It's fine love, don't try to speak, save your energy. I bent down and placed a kiss on her forehead. Her body lurched and I brought my eyes back to hers pleading with her to stay with me. She smiled, "He was wrong," she whispered as her eyes closed and I lost control. I began shaking her, begging her to wake up but it was no use. The pain had made her body shut down.

I looked back over at John, my eyes filled with tears, and watched him pummel that sick fuck. It wasn't enough though, I wanted to take his gun and shoot him. He was going to pay if anything happened to Liz.

"John," I called trying to control the sobs that wracked my body.

He looked up and his face fell. I knew what he was

thinking. I knew he thought Liz was gone. I shook my head to tell him no, to let him know she was still alive, if only just. I watched him take a deep breath, relieved before tightening his grip on the scumbag's neck.

"You son of a bitch, if she dies, I'll kill you myself, you hear?" he shouted.

Just then the door opened and two armed policemen entered.

"Put your hands in the air and step away from him," they ordered John.

"It's okay, officers, I'm the one who called you, this is the piece of filth you want," he said kicking my kidnapper in the gut.

"Please step away from him sir and place your hands in the air," the officer said again. "Let us do our job."

John moved aside as they pulled my kidnapper to his feet and held his hands behind his back. He didn't say anything, he just looked over at me and smiled. I couldn't help it, I let out a scream of frustration as I rocked Liz back and forth in my arms. The other police officer was at my side now, calling for backup on his radio. I was oblivious to what he was saying, my mind focused only on being with Liz, staying with her and keeping her safe. It's all I could do.

"Sir, I need you to let me look at her, Sir, I need to check her vitals, you're going to have to move. Sir.."

The raised voice seeped through and I looked up at him. "Save my wife I pleaded."

"Remember what I said Charlie boy, you'll know what it's like to lose everything."

His voice penetrated my mind. He enunciated each syllable of the word everything and as my eyes found his he grinned.

"You sick bastard, you'll pay for this," I shouted. I wanted to get up and rip his head off, but I couldn't move. I wouldn't. I was staying with Liz. She needed me to be strong for her now. I thought about everything she'd done for me, coming here to rescue me. What she must have been thinking, how scared she must have been. I thought of everything I'd been through over the past day, the terror of thinking she was lying dead on the beach. That's when I remembered my parents.

"Shit, my parents, they're being held captive. He has them," I shouted.

"It's okay Sir, just calm down and let us do our job. Your wife needs medical attention and fast or I'm afraid she won't make it. You need to apply as much pressure as you can, try and stop the bleeding. The chopper's on the way and should be here any minute."

His words stuck like a shard of glass piercing my heart.

*She won't make it.*

Oh, God what had I done? This was all my fault. He wanted me to suffer because I'd helped Susan. I was the one who should be lying in a pool of blood not Liz. She'd never harmed as much as a fly. She was caring and kind, and gentle, and she'd had enough shit of her own to deal with growing up. We were only getting past it, helping her to make her own decisions, and now here she was with a bullet in her. It's all my fault. I wanted to scream, to kick out, to throw a tantrum, but I couldn't. I couldn't do anything except pray and hope God would grant me a miracle. Had I earned a miracle? I didn't know, hell I wasn't even religious, but at that moment I would've been any religion, any person, if it meant saving her life.

I was a good guy, wasn't I? I'd never been on the bad side of the law and I'd worked hard to get where I was. There were no underhanded dealings, no dodgy investments. I'd done everything above board. Hell, I didn't even use my parent's money. I could have. I could have been the silver spooned kid who got everything because mommy and daddy had money and contacts, but I wanted to prove myself. I studied hard, went to college, and graduated top of my class. Sure, there'd been frat parties and booze and girls. I'm not saying I was a saint, but I didn't cheat my way to success. I had a knack for choosing the right stocks that's all. Call it a hunch or a gut instinct but I just knew where to invest and it paid off, got me to where I am today. But that's the thing, you see, I'd give it all up in a heartbeat if it meant saving Liz. She was my everything, my reason to get up in the morning, my smile, the light at the end of the day. My life was worthless without her. I may have money, but what's money without someone to share it with?

I hadn't planned on falling in love. Nah, not me. Love was for suckers and I wasn't going to let some woman interrupt my life. My perspective changed when I met Liz. I spotted her instantly. She looked so out of place, sitting by herself staring out the window of Luca's. Luca's was the coffee shop on South and main and my 1pm stop every day. I don't know what it was about her that caught my attention that first day. She was just sitting there staring out the window, her two hands wrapped around her cup oblivious to the world. Her dark curls were pulled back into a ponytail and she wore little or no makeup. She never moved, just sat there, and at exactly 1:25pm she up and left. I don't think she ever drank any of the coffee that sat in front of her. It happened again the next day and the day after that, the same routine over and over again.

After a week of watching this mysterious girl curiosity got the better of me. I placed my coffee down on her table and asked if I could sit. It took her a moment to acknowledge me and when she looked up with those big green eyes, I was lost.

Those massive emeralds pulled me in and looked right into my soul.

"Can I sit?" I asked again.

"Um, yes," she said looking around, her face flushed with embarrassment before she went back to staring out the window.

She never said another word that day and I sat fascinated by her beauty and the sadness that seemed to waft off her. It took another week before I got her to speak to me and that was just her name. She was so quiet and timid, almost afraid to speak, but I persisted. The first time she smiled I thought my chest would explode. Her whole face lit up and her eyes sparkled. She was beautiful, and when she laughed, my god, it was like summer, birds singing, the sun beaming down. She took my breath away and I knew in that instant that I wanted her for the rest of my life.

I finally realized that day what my mother had been trying to explain for years.

"Love comes at you like a bolt of lightning. You don't see it, but once it touches you, you won't ever want to let it go. It's a feeling deep inside that you can't explain. It makes you smile, makes you want to dance and do silly things and just the thought of losing it causes your whole world to become dark. Love is precious and those that are lucky enough to find it should always treasure it," she'd said.

Her words echoed in my mind as reality came flooding back. Tears streamed down my cheeks falling onto my blood-stained hands.

"Sir, the chopper's here, we need to take her now."

The officer's voice startled me and I looked up at him.

"Chopper's here, we're gonna get her to hospital now."

I nodded. It was all I could do as paramedics appeared

beside me armed with instruments and talking in rapid succession amongst themselves. I was lost. I could feel myself slipping away into the recesses of my mind. I couldn't cope with losing her and my mind was ensuring that I would escape this trauma.

"Hey, man, she's going to be fine. She's a tough girl, Liz."

I looked up, my vision blurred from my tears to see John standing beside me. He placed his hand on my shoulder and gave it a gentle squeeze.

"Come on, let's get you on that chopper."

I moved in a daze, unresponsive, uncaring, my mind drifting to happier times as Liz was strapped onto a gurney and airlifted out of our nightmare. The cops tried to ask questions, but I couldn't think straight, my mind was on Liz.

She was rushed straight into surgery once we arrived at the hospital, doctors and nurses rushed around her. It was like watching from a distance. All of this was happening but I was just a bystander, numb to the whole event. A nurse patched up the cut on my face and bandaged my wrists. She tried to hook me up to an IV, but when I refused she insisted that I drink and rehydrate my body.

I sat, desolate, waiting for the doctors to tell me if my life would resume or end in that hospital.

"She's gonna pull through you know," John said taking the seat beside me in the waiting room.

His head was bandaged but he looked okay.

"She's a fighter, Liz, the toughest woman I've ever met."

I looked up at him surprised by his statement and he must have seen it on my face.

"She thought you were dead you know, insisted on bringing your body home."

I looked at him, complete confusion on my face, but I

couldn't bring myself to speak. I was afraid if I opened my mouth I'd scream and never stop. The pain building inside my chest was unbearable as the thought of losing Liz started to suffocate me.

"That bastard left a life-like dummy in your place. She woke up on that beach thinking you'd died in her arms. When the guys found her she was hysterical. They brought her back to the ship. I thought she was an actress, honestly I did, and when she collapsed I took her straight here."

"What?" I gasped. *She thought I was dead? He thought she was an actress?*

"Yeah, we're doing a pirate reality documentary type thing," John said as if reading my thoughts. "We thought it was a surprise from the production team or something. Anyway, all she kept saying was 'Where's Charles'. To be honest, I thought she was nuts. The guys told me there was no one else on the beach."

"You bought her here?"

"Yeah, after she passed out. She had a concussion and was dehydrated. Didn't matter though, she insisted on going back to the island to bring your body home."

I smiled. I couldn't help it. My Liz, all brave and strong.

"She's tough, she'll make it," John continued.

"She is," was all I could say.

"Listen, Charles, I have to ask," John paused and I looked up at him giving him permission to continue. "Who's the Susan that lunatic kept going on about? I need to know who she was?"

I took a deep breath. Susan, my one good deed in life turned out to be my worst nightmare.

"It's okay, take your time," John said sensing my distress.

It didn't matter though. Nothing mattered now. Liz was in

surgery, my life was in tatters, and it all happened because I tried to do something good for someone. My mind raced over everything that had happened coming to an abrupt stop at my parents.

"Shit, my parents."

"They're fine, no harm done. They're on their way here, catching the next flight."

"How?"

"Cops sent a text saying you signed and to release them. They also sent back up to the hotel. The two guys holding your parents are already in custody and your parents are fine. They weren't harmed."

I took a deep breath relieved that my parents hadn't suffered because of me too. I'd caused all this mess and I knew it. Defeated I placed my head in my hands and closed my eyes. If only I could rewind time. I felt John's hand on my shoulder again.

"She's gonna get through this," he whispered. "I know she will."

*How could he know? Who the fuck was he anyway?*

I couldn't help it, I snapped. I lifted my head and looked right at him.

"How the fuck do you know?" I shouted.

"Hey, man, I get it, but I'm only trying to help, same way I helped Liz to save your ass," he said his hands in the air.

"Helped Liz, helped Liz, she got fucking shot. How the hell was that helping?" I roared before breaking down and sobbing like a baby.

The surgery doors opened then and Liz was wheeled out, hooked up to beeping machines with tubes coming out of everywhere. I jumped to my feet as the doctor came towards me.

My chest felt heavy, I couldn't catch my breath as I waited for him to deliver his news.

"Is she...?"

"Your wife is going to be fine, Mr. Parker. We've stopped the internal bleeding and there's no permanent damage. She's in an induced coma to give her body time to heal. She had a hairline fracture of the skull too, but we're confident she'll make a full recovery. Once she's settled you can sit with her."

His words washed over me like a warm shower, comforting and relaxing.

*She's alive. My Liz made it.*

Tears spilled out over my cheeks as I took in my first real breath in hours.

"See, I told you. She's a fighter your Liz."

John spoke from behind me and I turned to see him smiling.

"I'm sorry..." I muttered.

"No need. I'd have done the same. Now let's get you where you need to be."

I nodded and followed a nurse up to the ICU where Liz was being settled.

"Thank you, for helping her," I said as John turned to leave.

"How could I not? She's something special your Liz," he sighed. "I'll bring you a coffee and let the cops know where you are, they still have questions that I can't answer."

"Thanks John."

\*\*\*

The hours turned into days as I sat by Liz's bedside stroking my thumb gently across her hand, pleading with her to wake up. The cops had been and I'd answered their questions.

It turned out my kidnapper, Dominic Burns, had planned everything. He'd set the small explosion on the yacht making sure we were close enough to the shore that I'd survive. He'd drugged the champagne and had men waiting for my parents in their hotel. The police uncovered everything and he'd be facing a lot of jail time. He was completely deranged, convinced I was the reason Susan had left him. He couldn't believe that once she was clean she realized what a pig he really was and she decided herself that she didn't want anything to do with him.

John hadn't left the hospital either, insisting on waiting till Liz woke up. We chatted. He was a good man and without him I don't know what would have happened to Liz. I told him about Susan and how I'd helped her with her drug habit. Turns out, she was his sister.

My parents arrived unharmed and booked into a hotel nearby. They tried to get me to leave, have a shower, get cleaned up, but I refused. No one was taking me away from Liz ever again.

The nurses insisted I eat and drink or they were going to have me removed from the hospital. This was the only thing I agreed to.

The days passed and still no change. The constant beeping of machines my only companion as I sat and recounted all our precious memories. They say coma patients can hear you talking to them. I hope it's true.

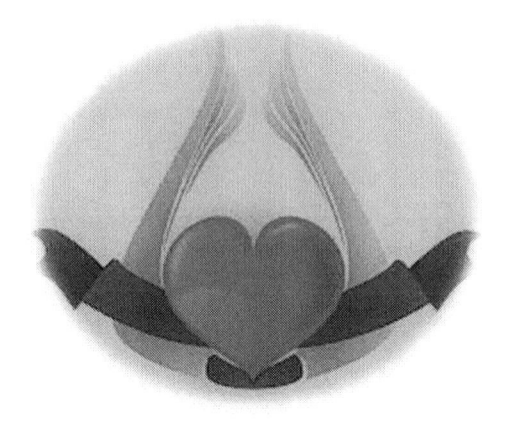

# LIZ

A beeping noise invaded the darkness and I felt someone holding my hand. I tried to move but my body wasn't responding. I was trapped in the darkness, alone, and frightened. The beeping noise was getting louder and I couldn't shut it out. My body felt heavy and I tried again to move, but it was like I was frozen. The darkness took my senses away again and there was nothing.

This happened over and over again. A few moments of sound, muffled voices, and always a hand holding mine, stroking it gently.

I heard it again, the beeping noise. It vibrated through me. There was a hand in mine again. I heard a voice. I heard talking, but it wasn't clear. I tried to think, tried to focus, but it was too hard. Then I heard it again.

"It's Charles, you need to wake up baby, you need to come back to me."

The mention of his name helped to clear the dark fog and I tried to move once more. My fingers twitched and I heard a gasp.

"Liz, Liz, wake up baby. It's me, Charles."

I tried to open my eyes, to move, but nothing was happening. I started to panic. I heard beeping, it was faster this time. Something was wrong. I couldn't move. I couldn't see. I tried to move my lips to call out his name but I was paralyzed.

"Liz, I'm here baby."

Charles sounded like he was in so much pain. What had I done? Why was I trapped in this darkness? The beeping was getting louder and I heard him shouting.

"She's waking up. She's waking up."

"I'm not. I can't," I shouted back in my head.

My sense of hearing was overwhelming. It was like someone turned up the volume whilst turning all my other senses off. I heard doors opening, feet rushing across the floor, but I was still in the dark.

"It's okay Liz. I'm here," Charles said squeezing my hand.

I felt it. It was the only thing keeping me calm. I moved my fingers again. They were reacting to his touch and squeezing back.

"Can you open your eyes baby?"

I tried, but it was useless, nothing was working. What happened to me? Memories of a monster and a gun began to flash through my mind and I felt my body react with the shock.

Oh, my god, I'd been shot. I remembered the agonizing

pain as the bullet forced its way through my stomach. I remembered Charles pleading with me not to die and the realization that my father had been wrong. He'd lied.

"Don't worry Mr. Parker, this can take some time. She'll come around when she's ready. All the signs are positive."

I didn't recognize the voice that spoke but I felt Charles relax. His fingers started stroking the back of my hand, moving up along my arm. He had such soft skin. I always wondered how he kept his hands so soft especially when he spent so much time sailing. Memories of our life together began to float through my mind as sleep took hold.

There was silence when I woke. Charles' hand was still in mine. It wasn't moving. I moved my fingers checking if they were still working. It didn't take as much effort this time. The darkness had lifted too and for the first time, I could see light behind my eyelids. I felt my breath going in and out of my body and I relaxed. I was really here this time.

My eyes fluttered open, a fraction at a time as the bright light assaulted them. I let them adjust before looking around. My gaze landed on Charles. He was asleep in the chair beside my bed. His eyes were puffy, his face gray. He looked so tired. His hair was a mess and dark waves hung over his forehead. I swallowed hard, my throat was so dry. I needed water. I squeezed Charles' hand again as I tried to say his name. My voice didn't come out. A dry croak was all I could manage. I watched Charles' eyelids peel back and his gaze find mine.

"Liz, oh Liz, you came back to me."

Tears filled his eyes as he leaned forward and his hands cupped my face.

"I thought I'd lost you."

I tried to speak again but the pain in my throat was too much.

"Don't move, I'll get the doctor."

He pressed a small button on the side of my bed and a nurse came flying into the room.

"She's awake," Charles said.

"That's wonderful, Mr. Parker. I'll just get the doctor."

She looked at me and smiled before she left.

I looked at the man gazing down at me, my man, my Charles. He was alive. I felt the tears flow down my cheeks.

"Don't cry love, you'll be fine. We'll be fine. We're together again and no one will ever separate us," he said, his tears falling too.

The nurse arrived back with the doctor. He moved closer to my bed a smile on his face too. He pulled out a light pointing it into my eyes and asking me to follow it. He checked my temperature, took my blood pressure, and wrote things on a clipboard. My eyes never left Charles.

"Are you in any pain?" the doctor asked.

I pointed to my throat. I needed water.

"Ah yes," he said. "You'll have a sore throat for a few days. We had to place you on a ventilator to help you breathe."

He turned to the nurse. "Can you get Mrs. Parker some water please?"

Mrs. Parker. It was the first time I'd heard myself called that with Charles sitting beside me. I smiled. The nurse handed Charles a beaker of water and a straw.

"Small sips only," she said.

The water felt like heaven. I was so thirsty. The doctor explained that I'd been shot but no permanent damage had been caused. He said a lot more but my mind drifted and sleep took over. Charles' voice was the last thing I heard.

"Sleep my love, I'll be right here. You're not alone."

I woke to a sight I would never tire of, my Charles. He was

asleep and I took my time taking in how handsome the man before me was. He must have felt my stare because his eyes opened and the biggest smile I'd ever seen spread across his face.

"Hey you," I smiled.

"Hey yourself, how you feeling today?"

"I'm okay," I said. "What happened?"

Charles took a deep breath. I knew this was painful for him but I had to know. He nodded his understanding and cleared his throat.

"After you were shot and you fell into my arms John knocked that monster to the ground. The police heard the gunshot and barged into the cabin moments later. They rushed you here and you had to have emergency surgery. Everything's okay though, there was no permanent damage. They placed you in this room on a ventilator to give your body time to recover and I haven't left your side since."

"I'm sorry," I blurted out as my eyes filled with tears.

"God no Liz. I'm sorry. This was all my fault. He was after me."

I stared at Charles confused.

He took a deep breath and cleared his throat. "Five years ago I helped a young girl. She'd broken into my apartment. She was a drug addict and I helped her to get clean, start a new life. If I hadn't done that, none of this would have happened. It's all my fault you got shot, Liz. It's my fault you almost died," he said placing his head in his hands.

"Charles you did a good thing helping that girl."

"No Liz, I didn't. I may have helped her but I didn't save her. He found her, tortured her for years, made people think she was crazy, and then he killed her."

I gasped. "What do you mean?"

"He told me during the whole kidnapping ordeal. He told me I'd taken everything from him and he would make me pay. He said I would know what it was like to have everyone I love taken from me, that I would know the greatest despair. He almost succeeded Liz, he had my parents and he told me he'd killed you, left you dead on the beach."

"But he didn't," I said smiling. "He didn't win Charles." I cleared my throat, I needed to know everything. "This girl," I said looking deep into his eyes. "Who was she?"

"Her name was Susan. She got away from him but he found her. He tormented her made her think she was going mad. In the end, he gave her a choice him or death. He planned to kill her if she didn't go back to him. She chose death and jumped off a building."

"Susan," I muttered my brain processing all the information. "Oh my God, John," I shouted. "John's sister Susan."

Charles nodded lowering his eyes in shame.

"Where is he?" I asked.

"He's here. He hasn't left either."

"I'd like to see him, thank him," I said.

"I'll get him," Charles said rising from the chair. "He's been waiting."

Moments later John appeared at my door.

"Hey Liz, how you feeling?"

"John, I'm so sorry." My tears were spilling out over my cheeks now as I thought of the pain he must be going through. The guilt he felt over his sister. Did he know the truth now?

He walked towards me and took my hand. "You have nothing to be sorry about you hear. If it wasn't for you I would never have found out what happened to Susan. Now I know," he swallowed. "I promised her I'd find out what happened. I promised her I wouldn't rest until I did. Now I know. Now I know why."

He lowered his head and I knew he was thinking about her. I knew he was angry that he didn't believe her and had her committed. I squeezed his hand hoping to give him some comfort.

"She understood John, and you did a good thing, you protected her from him while she was in the hospital. It wasn't your fault."

"I know that now and she can finally rest in peace knowing the truth has finally been uncovered."

I looked up at him, the towering strength above me. Without him, I would have died on that beach thinking Charles was dead too.

"Thank you," I said

He didn't need to say anything. The look we shared said it all. He smiled and looked at Charles. "You keep her safe, she's one hell of a lady."

Charles smiled. "You can bet your life I will."

John turned back to me. "You take care now, and if you ever need anything you just call."

I swallowed the sobs threatening to escape. "Where are you going now?"

"I've got a pirate show to complete," he winked.

I laughed for the first time in what seemed like forever. Charles stood and they both shook hands.

"You keep in touch," Charles said. "And if you ever need anything, you just let us know."

John left and I felt a peace settle over my hospital room. Charles sat beside me and we just gazed at each other.

"What happened to the man that shot me? Who was he?"

"His name was Dominic Burns and he won't be bothering

us again love. The police took him away and he'll be serving a long time believe me. It's not just the kidnapping and attempted murder changes, they have him for the torment he put Susan through, as well as being the cause of her death."

I looked down. I still couldn't believe this was all over.

"You don't need to worry about anything. You're safe now and I'll never let anything happen to you."

I moved my gaze to his and smiled. I knew he meant it.

"Liz?"

"hmmm."

"What did you mean when you said, he was wrong, you know just before you passed out in my arms?"

My eyes dropped to the bed. "My father," I swallowed. "He always told me I'd die alone, that without him I was nothing."

I looked back up at Charles, my eyes meeting his. I wanted to see what he was thinking before I continued. "He was wrong, he lied. You were with me. I was never alone."

"I'll never leave you, Liz. You are my strength. You are my life and you are the strongest person I've ever known. Your father and what he did to you," he stopped. "We'll deal with that when you're ready."

Charles lowered his head to mine and we sat nose to nose, eyes to eyes, feeling the love between us before he let his lips slowly caress mine.

"I love you," he whispered. "Thank you for rescuing me."

"I love you too, you not only rescued me, you brought me back to life."

His lips brushed against mine and his arms wrapped firmly around my body pulling me closer to him. He was never going to let me go. I smiled and deepened the kiss letting my tongue sweep across his bottom lip, begging for entrance. He obliged and my tongue thrust inside his mouth craving the connection that has been broken by that mad man. I needed to taste him, to feel him with every part of my being. I wanted him to know that I was his. His soft moan told me he understood. I knew in that moment that I was truly alive and the demons from my past would never hold me back again. I was Liz Parker and I was ready to live my life with the man I loved and the man I knew loved me. I'd found my forever.

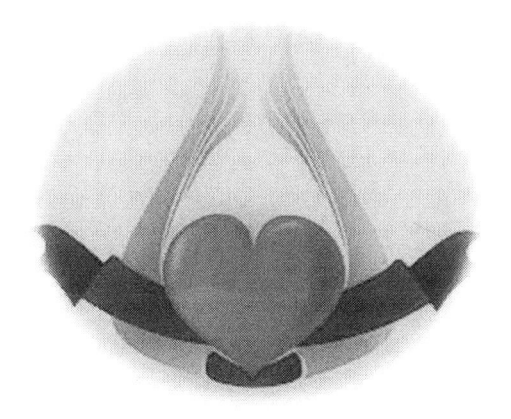

## EPILOGUE – JOHN

I'd avoided the city like the plague for the past two years, lived my life under a dark cloud of guilt, and now I didn't know what to do. When the approval came for my pirates' documentary/reality show I'd been apprehensive. If I accepted it meant stepping back into the past and I wasn't sure if I was ready to face that cruel torment.

Susan was my younger sister. It was my job to look out for her and keep her safe. I hadn't done a very good job and when the police told me she killed herself I shut myself off from the world. My baby sister had pleaded with me to save her from the monster she said was chasing her, but I didn't believe her, no one did. The doctors insisted it was all in her head, remnants of her drug abuse. They said she was unstable and a danger to herself. I agreed and had her committed. She thanked me, said she was safe. I thought she was fine, the medication and the counselling had worked. Two weeks out of hospital and she plunged six stories to the ground. It was my fault. I should have listened to her. I should have believed her. I failed her.

Stepping back into the city, into the place of my nightmares was harder than I thought, but I'd worked so hard to get the funding for my show. If I turned it down now, I'd never get it again.

Strange how fate works isn't it? I'd promised Susan I'd find the truth and now that I had I didn't know what to do with it. Liz reminded me so much of her. The determination and the strength of her conviction. She was adamant Charles' body was on that beach. No one believed her, the doctors looked at her with that same look, the pity that leaks out of them. Mental illness is a curse no one should have to face, but when she looked at me and pleaded for my help, I saw my baby sister and in that moment, I couldn't say no. In that moment, I swore that I wouldn't make the same mistake again, and I didn't.

I'd kept my promise to Susan. I'd found out what really happened to her and now Dominic Burns would pay. He'd pay for taking my sister's life.

Just thinking about that sorry excuse for a human being had me clenching my fists and I smiled knowing I'd knocked the smirk off his face. It had felt good to feel my fist crush his nose, that cracking sound of bone breaking was pure heaven to my ears.

"That one's for you sis," I'd whispered as I drew back for another punch.

I hadn't known the full truth then, not like I do now, but my instinct had been right. The way he'd said her name, the way he'd gloried in giving her a choice. What fucking choice, death or him? Susan hadn't killed herself, she'd saved herself, and now it was my turn. I'd lived under this cloud of doom for two years and my sun was finally breaking through. For the first time in a long time I could feel the heat on my face and I welcomed it.

As I pushed through the hospital exit doors I took in a deep breath and smiled. The first real smile I'd smiled since the day I put Susan's body in the ground. It was time to live, my time to live, and I planned on doing it to the full.

The End

# ABOUT THE AUTHOR

I am a freelance writer, poet, and author. I live in Co. Meath, Ireland with my husband and two children. I am known locally by my married name, Donnelly, but I write under my maiden name of Evans. I have been published in a number of magazines and journals in 2016. I am also the author of Surviving Suicide: A Memoir from Those Death Left Behind, published in 2012. When I'm not writing for work clients, I am usually reading the latest novels from some of the amazing indie authors out there, or sharing snippets from my latest manuscripts with my husband and children.

I've always loved writing. My passion began at a very young age and I wrote my first book at the age of 9. Writing this full-length novella is my first step into the fiction publishing world and while I'm nervous, I'm also very excited. This has been my dream for so long and to finally have the courage to pen stories and publish them is something I always wanted to do. Finding Forever began as a prompt from my writers' group. Our prompt was "pirates" and I wrote the first 1,000 words ending where Liz finds herself on the pirate ship. It sat idle on my laptop for almost a year before I picked it up again. I was doing a page a day challenge and decided that for the month I would work on finishing some of the pieces in my "to be completed" file on my computer. Little did I know when I picked up my pen to work on this that it would turn into a novella. The twists and turns that Finding Forever takes were a total surprise to me. I hadn't planned the story. I hadn't even thought it was going to be any more than a short story. The moment when I wrote about cameras, I knew something wonderful was about to happen. When I write, I allow the characters to tell me their story. I don't plan things out. I just let the story tell itself. I am so pleased with the initial beta reader response to this story and that is what encouraged me to publish it.

I am currently working on a new novel, the title of which is "Save Her Soul". This novel is a paranormal romance and I'm enjoying getting to know the characters. My main character, Kate, is stubborn and very feisty and I'm sure you'll love her as much as I do. I've included a sneak peak of Chapter 1 at the end of this book if you want to read it. I am hoping to have it finished by March 2017 with publication in the summer of 2017.

Also, included at the end of this book is "Mistletoe Magic" a short romantic Christmas story I wrote at the end of 2016.

If you'd like to keep up to date with what I'm working on, you can find more information on my website:
http://www.amandajevans.com
and on Facebook:
http://www.facebook.com/amandajevanswriter

Thank you so much for taking the time to read Finding Forever. I hope you've enjoyed it and if you have the time, I would really appreciate it if you could leave a review.

# SAVE HER SOUL
## CHAPTER 1

It all began with the flicker of a lighter, a cigarette reaching down into the flames. I don't know why I was mesmerized by this. I should have run; I should have hidden in the shadows but something about this man dressed in black had me intrigued. No one ever came out here. This was my place, my sanctuary and finding someone else here had never happened before. What did he want? How did he find this place? I thought I was the only one who came here. No, I knew I was the only one who came here. Nearly a year had passed and not one other soul had visited this grave site.

The flame died and he placed the lighter in his pocket. The cigarette moved to his lips and he sucked in a deep breath before exhaling. The smoke danced from his mouth forming perfect circles. Who was he? I thought about clearing my throat, asking him what he was doing in my place, but something told me not to. Instead I stood, silent, frozen to the spot, my eyes the only thing that moved. I watched him finish his cigarette then flick it to the ground. His black leather boots crushed it in a twisting motion. He never once looked in my direction. He just nodded to the darkness and left. I stood for what felt like minutes before moving to the spot he had vacated. I looked behind to where I had been standing. I would have been clearly visible to him. Why didn't he see me, acknowledge my existence? Perhaps he had. I followed his trail, down past the old train yard, out through the broken fence but there was nothing, no sign of anyone. Shrugging my shoulders, I turned and made my way home.

If he comes to my place again, I'll be having words. No one is taking it from me. It's mine and I will fight for it. I will fight for the only bit of peace I have left in this world. I need it. I need to be there, to feel her, to remember who she was and how I failed her. My sanctuary is my punishment and I will live with it until I get revenge and retribution for her life. I promised her and I keep my promises. Always.

I pushed open the door to my apartment. I call it an apartment but it's only two rooms with everything I need squashed in. It's all I can afford right now, but it won't be for long. As soon as I get my revenge I'll leave. I'll be ready then.

Sighing, I placed my coat across the back of the sofa. It wasn't much and the cushions were worn, but it was comfortable and that's all the mattered. It sat in the middle of the floor, a small wooden coffee table to the side, and a stove in front of it. I didn't use the stove often; I was used to the cold. In the corner of the room was the door to my bedroom. I'd say I slept there but I'd be lying. I didn't sleep much these days. I tossed and turned fighting against the nightmares and memories that consumed me. A small kitchen area to the left completed my little home. I flicked the switch on the kettle. I needed tea and time to think. The man in black had me spooked. Who was he? Did he work for Merlin? Was he spying on me? I replayed the events over and over as the kettle boiled. He didn't seem to notice me. He didn't look in my direction and I'd never seen him before. Maybe he was just there having a cigarette. Maybe he was lost. All the questions weren't doing me any good. I had no answers anyway. I made my tea and sat on the sofa. The warm liquid instantly calmed me as I sat back to contemplate my next move. I looked at the pile of papers spread out over the coffee table. I'd been tracking Merlin's movements, following members of his gang. I needed to find a way to get to him and get him alone so I could enact my revenge. He was going to suffer. He was going to feel the pain that he'd inflicted on Sarah. The thought of her brought tears to my eyes. Her bruised and bloodied body, destroyed when I found her. She'd pleaded for me to forgive her, said she couldn't stop them, before she closed her eyes for the last time.

I shook my head.

*Stop it, you're just tormenting yourself. You need to focus.*

I placed my tea on the table and reached for my notebook. I needed to jot down all the details of this mysterious man in black. If he was involved in all of this I had the upper hand. He didn't see me. I wrote down every detail I could remember. The circles of smoke he blew out, the biker style leather boots that he used to crush the cigarette. It was dark. The glow from the cigarette as he pulled on it had revealed a straight nose and hair that hung in his face but that was all. I knew I wouldn't recognize him if I saw him in daylight. If he was working for Merlin, I'd never know. I threw my notebook down.

"This is bloody useless. I'm getting nowhere. Whoever this guy is, if I see him again I'm gonna say something. I'm not a coward anymore."

I finished my tea and decided to call it a night. There was nothing more I could do and my head was throbbing as it was.

I tossed and turned all night. Memories of Sarah, her smile, her laughter, and of course the way I found her battered and bruised. My nightmares always ended the same way, Sarah's eyes pleading with me and begging me to help her. The sweat dripped down my face as I bolted upright in my bed. I grabbed the glass of water from my nightstand and guzzled it down. My throat was raw another sign that I had been crying and screaming in my sleep again. As the last remnants of my nightmare faded I looked at the picture of Sarah and me that sat beside my bed. We both looked so happy. The photo was taken two summers ago before all this mess happened, before Merlin, before Tommy, and before my life fell apart.

"I promise," I said as I kissed my palm and placed it over her smiling face.

My alarm announced that it was time to get up. I don't know why I even bothered to set it anymore. I was always awake. I dragged myself out of bed and into the shower. Work kept my mind busy and it was exactly what I needed. I worked in Kelly's Diner, two blocks away. It was only a waitressing job but the hours suited. The early morning shift was always busy and my lack of sleep meant I was always on time. Working from 5am to 1pm gave me the rest of the day to trace leads and my evenings were free to follow Merlin's scumbags to see what they were up to. The file I compiled was extensive. I could go to the police, but what was the point. The evidence I wanted, needed, to prove Sarah was murdered by Merlin was still out of reach. Until I had that, I was in limbo. I watched from the shadows, taking note of everything. I'd tried to be the hero. I confronted Merlin and his men not long after I'd found Sarah. The rage I'd felt was out of control and I paid dearly for it. It didn't matter that I was a woman, those men took joy in leaving me in a heap outside the abandoned warehouse on 4th street. I suffered broken ribs, a hairline fracture of my skull, and more bruises than I could count. This is what I got for letting my rage get the better of me. It won't happen again. Next time I'll be ready and then we'll see who is left lying on the ground bleeding.

It had taken some time to find Luke's but it was worth it. Luke's gym allowed me to train and work my body. I could take my rage out on the punch bag. Luke was a master of many arts and he was more than happy to train me. Each day it was something different, boxing, karate, you name it, he'd studied it and he was one hell of a teacher too. He thought me how to use my anger and channel my pain into a force that I could use. One year on and I knew I was nearly ready to take down Merlin and fulfil my promise to Sarah. Just a couple more weeks and I'd have everything in place.

I smiled as I walked through the door of Kelly's. This would all be over soon. I loved how quiet it was in the diner at this time of the morning. Flicking on the lights and the switch for the coffee machine I made my way into the back kitchen to get things ready for Armand. Armand was the best chef in the county and he was what put Kelly's on the map. Why he chose to stay here and not get a job in the big city was beyond me. I'd asked him once and his reply was 'love'. I scoffed. I'd be gone to the city in a heartbeat if I had his talents. He was headhunted all the time but always refused. He said he loved the country air and that he'd feel trapped in the city. I tried arguing that with all the money he'd make he could travel to the country whenever he wanted. He wasn't convinced and I dropped it. I smiled as I remembered all our little chats this past year. I'd miss him when I was gone. I brushed away the thought and busied myself filling milk jugs and setting out the condiments and menu boards on all the tables. The smell of fresh coffee filled the air as I glanced at the clock and made my way to the front door. Turning the sign to open I stepped back as it swung open and the little bell above jingled. My first customer of the day. I lifted my head ready with a beaming grin only to find Malcolm Merlin's lackey John Tidsdale standing in front of me. My stomach turned and I had to force down the snarl that wanted to escape my mouth.

"Morning Kate, you're looking good," he smirked.

I nodded. I couldn't bring myself to say anything. All I could think about was the two weeks I'd spent in the hospital after him and his goons had worked me over. Of course, they got away with it. My word against theirs and they had an alibi.

"Not talking to me, eh?" he said watching me closely.

I knew I had to play it cool, pretend to be the scared little woman he expected. I swallowed hard.

"Take a seat John, I'll be with you in a minute."

That did the trick. He smiled and made his way to a booth.

*Pull yourself together. You'll blow everything if you lose it now.*

My inner voice was right. I'd come too far to let my plans fall apart because of Tidsdale. I pulled the small notebook from my apron and followed him to his booth.

"What can I get you?" I asked adding a slight quiver to my voice. He had to think I was afraid even if I did want to smash his face in. I took a deep breath as he smiled at his menu.

"I'll have pancakes and coffee. I'm celebrating this morning," he winked.

That could only mean trouble I thought as I answered as sweetly as I could.

"Sure, I'll bring the coffee straight over. Armand's just arrived so the pancakes will be a few minutes."

I felt his hand on my arm as he stopped me from leaving. God, I wanted so much to turn and knock the cheesy grin off his face.

"How've you been Kate? Haven't seen you round, since you know," he raised his eyebrows, baiting me.

"Busy," I scowled and turned to leave.

This time I moved fast or I knew my temper wouldn't hold.

I heard him chuckle as I left.

Oh, what I wouldn't do to add a little bit of arsenic to his coffee and kill the fucker right here, right now.

I shook my head. I couldn't. My mind replayed our conversation as I made his coffee. Celebrating. What was he celebrating and what were they up to? Things had been quiet over at the warehouse of late. That was not a good sign. Terrible in fact. When the warehouse was quiet it usually meant, Merlin was out of town, but not this time. I'd seen him two nights ago outside Club B. They were up to something.

With coffee in hand I made my way back to Tidsdale. He was on the phone, but the conversation halted as soon as I arrived. I did manage to catch a few words though.

"All quiet…yep…gotcha…8.30…right boss."

"Your coffee," I said placing the steaming cup beside him.

"Thanks, Kate."

I turned and was once again halted in my tracks.

"By the way, you might want to give training a miss tonight. The boss has something in mind for Luke," he laughed.

I froze and my head turned at his words. My hands fisted at my sides. I glared at him.

"You touch him and you'll be sorry," I spat.

"Oh now aren't you the feisty one? Thought you might have learned your lesson last time. Not to worry, boss said I can have you all to myself if you ever try anything again." He licked his lips, "I'm hoping you do."

My stomach dropped and my hands started shaking. They knew. They fucking knew and he was baiting me. The way he licked his lips and the look he gave me sent shivers down my spine. I stomped off to the kitchen. I needed to calm myself.

"You alright Kate?" Armand asked seeing my hands shake and the red in my cheeks.

"Yeah," I muttered berating myself silently for my slip up. If they knew I was training with Luke, what else did they know? My mind was like a whirlwind. I took a deep breath to focus.

*You're in work. Calm down. You can sort this later. Don't give Tidsdale any more than you already have.*

"Those pancakes ready?" I asked Armand.

"Yes, here you go,"

I grabbed the plate as Armand placed his hand on my arm.

"Kate, you know I'm here if you need anything, right?"

"I know, thanks Armand." I said swallowing the lump in my throat.

Armand was one of a kind, so giving. He was my rock and he'd helped me out so much after Sarah, but I couldn't tell him what I was doing though. I couldn't put him or his family in danger. This was my fight and I would face Merlin alone. I had been gathering evidence for months now. The police couldn't help when Sarah died but when I'd finished they'd have all the evidence they needed to put his gang away for a long time. Merlin, he was mine. He wasn't going to prison. He was going to hell.

Pushing through the kitchen doors I made my way back to Tidsdale. I placed the pancakes in front of him and turned to leave.

"Remember what I said Kate, gym's off limits today so don't you do anything stupid."

I huffed.

*Gym's off limits, I'd go if I wanted and he wouldn't stop me.*

"Course you can go if you like. I'd love to see that cute body of yours all sweaty."

The tone in his voice made my stomach sick and I marched across the diner, anything to get away from him.

The rest of my shift went without incident. Tidsdale ate and left, grinning at me as he did. The usual morning rush arrived after him and my shift flew by. Before long it was one, and time for me to find out exactly what was going on. I knew Merlin controlled the Glades but I was sure Luke wasn't involved in any way. He was training me to fight. He knew Sarah was murdered. My mind replayed conversation after conversation from the past 9 months. I'd never mentioned Merlin or my plan for revenge and neither had he. He'd asked more than once what I planned to do with my life, told me I needed focus, but I never answered. I always shook my head and went back to attacking the punch bag.

My heart was racing fearing he was involved, that he was in league with Merlin. I tried to push it away, convince myself that I was wrong, but the sinking feeling in my gut told me I wasn't. I had a decision to make. Did I pretend to be the weak kitten Tidsdale assumed I was and stay away? Or show them the fierce tiger I'd become? They knew I'd been training, but how much did they know? I was rattled that was for sure and the only way I knew to calm myself and think clearly was to talk to Sarah.

I'd been so distracted I hadn't even noticed I'd been walking in the direction of her death site, but once there I felt her energy wash over me. I sank to the ground and placed my hand on the blood-stained concrete.

"Tell me what to do?" I whispered. "I need you Sarah."

I let the tears come. This was the only place I cried. The only place I allowed my grief to take over. With my head buried in my hands I let my sobs out. The pain was still so raw. The images of her tortured body. I still didn't know why, but I knew one way or the other I wasn't leaving this world without getting answers.

I sat there in silence remembering everything. The fight Sarah and I had. How she said she hated me. I was only looking out for her. She was all I had, my baby sister, and I was supposed to protect her. I was supposed to keep her safe. I failed. I hadn't been there. We fought that night. I pleaded with her not to go out, not to see Tommy but she wouldn't listen. She told me I didn't control her life and she was right, but she didn't know what I did. Tommy wasn't the guy she thought he was. He was in way over his head with Merlin and he was dragging her down too. No matter what I said she didn't listen. She was blinded by her infatuation with him. She said they were in love, that there were getting out of town, moving north where they could be together. They had it all planned and I could still see the excitement in her eyes as she replayed the perfect life she was going to have.

"Come with us," she'd said. "You can stay with us, move college. You're welcome to stay with us as long as you like, sis."

I don't know why I didn't listen and pack my bags. We could have left; we could've gone that night and she'd still be alive. It was all my fault.

"I'm so sorry Sarah," I cried. "I didn't mean it, I love you."

My body was wracked with grief as I tried to escape my memories. I couldn't do this, not now, now yet. I had to be strong. I had to be strong for Sarah.

Shaking my head and clearing my throat, I looked up to the sky as I made my vow, my promise.

"I will make them pay."

I felt better. I had focus again and that was exactly what I needed if my plan was going to work.

A clicking sound caught my attention and I looked up. It was him. The man in black. The clicking sound was his cigarette lighter. I watched as he placed the cigarette to his lips. The smell of smoke filled the air. There were no circles this time just a long stream of smoke leaving his mouth. I felt my blood boil. How dare he come here? This was my place, mine. I stood ready for a fight.

"What the hell do you think you're doing? I shouted.

He didn't move, didn't even flinch.

"I said, what are you doing?"

"And I heard you, I just chose not to answer."

His voice was soft but masculine. I found it calming and sultry and I had to shake my head.

"This is my place; you're not welcome here."

He looked straight at me now and his eyes found mine, deep pools of blue connecting with my brown pits of despair. I took in a deep breath. His eyes were mesmerizing like they could see through me into my very soul.

"It's an alleyway. I don't think you can own an alleyway," he smirked.

I gulped. I couldn't think straight.

"Yes, well I do," I managed to spit out.

"Hmm, I see," he smiled taking another long drag out of his cigarette before tossing to the ground and squashing it with his boot.

My eyes followed his movements then back up to his face. He nodded at me then turned and left.

"Wait, hold on. What were you doing here? Did Merlin send you?" I shouted after him.

He didn't stop. He didn't look behind. He just walked around the corner.

"Shit," I shouted as I ran to follow him.

I turned the corner, but he was gone, vanished, no trace of him, just like last time. This was a little freaky, but I shrugged it off. He's a fast mover I told myself as dread filled me. Maybe he was spying on me? Maybe he was working for Merlin and they knew exactly what I was up to? I had to make sure my Intel was safe and I had to do it now.

I headed for home, watching, keeping my eyes peeled for any followers. My life depended on making sure that the evidence I'd collected over the last 9 months was safe. It was my payback. It was going to put Merlin's men in prison and give me the chance to take my revenge on Merlin and that involved a lot of blood.

\*\*\*

To Be Published in Summer 2017

# MISTLETOE MAGIC

Cassie Blake stood outside Ivy House debating with herself. A mammoth task lay waiting for her inside and she didn't want to face it.

"Hey Cass, you set for tonight?"

Stephanie's cheery voice interrupted her thoughts, and she jumped as she turned to see her friend making her way up the driveway.

Cassie shrugged her shoulders, "Still debating," she sighed.

"Oh, no you don't Cassie Blake, the whole town is counting on you. It's tradition, and it's your turn."

"I know Steph, but I can't do it. I hate Christmas. You know that."

"That's bull," Stephanie snapped. "And besides, it's not Christmas you hate, it's Ben and you need to snap out of it. It's been two years Cass, and a good party is just what you need. Oh, and did I mention Jake's coming home especially?"

Cassie glared at her friend. She was in no mood for her matchmaking.

"He's bringing his new girlfriend," Stephanie added with a smirk. "I'll be back in an hour to help with the decorating, got to pop into the office."

Cassie went to object but Stephanie turned and marched down the driveway.

"One hour and you better be ready," she called over her shoulder.

Cassie sighed and made her way into the house and the box of decorations waiting for her on the dining room table.

The Christmas party was something the residents in Summerfield looked forward to and if she was honest, she'd always enjoyed them too. Each year the party was held in a different house. The last time she'd been the host was five years ago.

"Well, it's now or never," Cassie muttered pulling open the box and peering inside. She couldn't help but smile as she pulled garlands and lights out onto the table. The ornaments had been in her family for generations and she lined them up ready to be placed in their appointed locations. Each had its own special place, just the way they had for her grandmother and mother before her.

*Maybe it won't be so bad. After all, Christmas used to be fun.*

Reaching into the bottom of the box Cassie pulled out a small piece of velvet cloth. She dropped it. She knew what it was. The mistletoe, her grandmother's favorite piece and the cause of her misery.

'You'll meet the man of your dreams under this mistletoe,' her grandmother had said. That's how she met grandpa and how mom met dad. Cassie smiled as she remembered her grandmother's tales of love and the magic mistletoe. They'd always been so special and real until she met Ben. She'd kissed him under that very same mistletoe five years ago and all she'd gotten was a broken heart and a mountain of debt.

"Not this year, grandma," she said as she closed the box. "No more magic for me."

The next hour flew by as Cassie placed ornaments and decorations around the house. True to her word Stephanie arrived to help, and the day passed in laughter, music, and the odd glass of wine. When Stephanie asked about grandma's magic mistletoe Cassie lied and said she couldn't find it.

At 5pm the caterers arrived to set up the food. The decorating was almost complete, and the house looked amazing. Cassie caught Stephanie looking at the blank space above the living room door where the mistletoe hung each year. She saw the disappointment on her face but refused to budge. There would be no mistletoe this year.

"I'm just going to put this box upstairs then I'm off to beautify myself," Stephanie called out as she grabbed the empty decorations box from the dining room.

"Thanks, Steph, don't know what I would've done without you today," Cassie said looking at up at her friend as she placed the last bauble on the tree and switched on the lights. She couldn't help but smile. Everything looked amazing, and she was looking forward to the party.

"I'll be back at seven," Stephanie said as she opened the front door. "Be ready."

"I will," Cassie smiled.

The house was filled with the scent of mince pies and mulled wine.

"I'm going to have fun tonight," she whispered to herself as she made her way upstairs to change.

Dressed and ready as she would ever be, Cassie took a deep breath and made her way downstairs. The blank space over the dining room door caught her eye. Normally the mistletoe hung there to catch any unsuspecting guests. Of course, everyone in Summerfield knew about her grandmother's mistletoe and the stories that came with it. Cassie chewed on her bottom lip, a nervous habit, and sighed. What would she tell everyone? I could just put it up and tell Stephanie I found it she thought, but then shrugged her shoulders.

"No, not this year. I don't want any more of that mistletoe magic in my life."

Cassie made her way to the kitchen and filled a large glass with mulled wine before making her way to the living room to set up the music playlist for the evening. Before long festive favorites were playing and Cassie began to relax.

At seven neighbors and friends started to arrive and Cassie spent the next hour chatting and mingling. Her house was open to everyone and people came and went as they pleased. It's the way it was every year. No one noticed the missing mistletoe. Stephanie arrived at eight, later than promised, but she looked stunning.

"Hey Cass, sorry I'm late. I was waiting for Jake and Melissa."

With that, Jake pushed his way around her and smothered Cassie in a hug. He was like her own little brother too and she couldn't help but laugh as he swung her in the air.

"Looking great Cass," he smiled.

"You too," she beamed, "and I hear you brought a guest."

"Yep, this is Mel," he said pulling a petite brunette from behind Stephanie. "Mel, this is Cassie, my surrogate big sis."

"Pleased to meet you, I hope you enjoy your stay here in Summerfield," Cassie said extending her hand to Mel in greeting.

"Thanks for letting me crash your party. Jake's told me lots of stories about the three of you." Mel said shaking her hand.

"Hopefully all good," Cassie said as she smiled. She liked this girl and from the look on Jake's face, she knew he really liked her too.

"You didn't find the mistletoe then?" Stephanie interrupted looking at the blank space above the door.

Cassie felt her face blush, but she stuck to her lie. "No sign of it," she said.

"Right," Stephanie smirked.

Cassie looked away. She knew Stephanie was on to her. She always knew when Cassie lied.

"Well, have a great time you two, food and drink is in the kitchen" she said to Jake and Mel while grabbing Stephanie by the arm and pulling her aside.

"What's with the smirk?" she asked.

"Oh, nothing. I'm going to get a drink you want one?"

Cassie shook her head, "Fine I'll have a glass of mulled wine."

The evening was going well. Friends and neighbors were chatting, and the food was going down a treat. Cassie was deep in conversation with Margaret Tyrell, the local real estate agent when a stranger caught her attention. He was tall with dark hair.

"That's Agnes' nephew in from the city for a couple of days," Margaret informed her. "Come on I'll introduce you. He's quite the catch."

"Oh, there's no need," Cassie exclaimed embarrassed that she'd been caught staring at him.

"Nonsense dear, you've been single far too long."

Cassie took in a deep breath. She knew there was no way of getting out of it. She followed Margaret across the room.

"Yoo-hoo David, I want you to meet our host Cassie Blake," she called as they crossed the room.

Cassie watched the handsome stranger turn and smile at them. He was really something, deep blue eyes and dark hair that fell over his forehead. As if feeling her gaze, he ran his fingers through his hair. Cassie sighed. She'd sworn off men. She was still trying to fix the mess Ben left her with and she'd lost faith in the opposite sex.

"David, this is Cassie," Margaret beamed.

"Pleasure to meet you, Cassie," he said extending his hand.

"Tut, tut, David, it's Christmas and you know here in Summerfield we don't extend our hand, give her a kiss on the cheek, she doesn't bite, I promise," Margaret butted in.

Cassie felt her cheeks blush and if she wasn't mistaken, there was a slight redness to David's too as he leaned forward and kissed her on the cheek.

"Pleasure to meet you," he whispered against her ear as he pulled away.

"You too," was all Cassie could manage. His sultry voice had gotten to her.

"Well, I'll leave you two to chat," Margaret announced calling out to Sarah Pearson who'd just passed by.

"She's something else, isn't she?" Cassie asked breaking the silence.

David gazed into her eyes. "That's what I love about this place, everyone's so friendly."

"I haven't seen you around before," Cassie said knowing she'd never forget his face.

"It's been a while," he sighed. "Can I get you a drink?"

"Sure, everything's in the kitchen," Cassie said.

David looked towards the kitchen and then back at Cassie. "I'll meet you back here, don't go anywhere."

He smiled and Cassie felt her face blush again. He was gorgeous and that voice, she could listen to it forever. A few minutes later David arrived back with two glasses of wine.

"It's a lovely place you've got here Cassie."

"Thanks, it's always been in the family. What about you, where do you live?"

The conversation flowed and Cassie found herself laughing and smiling. She'd caught Stephanie watching them a couple of times but she was having too much fun to pay her any attention. David worked in finance in the city. He was single, and he spent most of his time working. He was in Summerfield to help his aunt Agnes while his uncle Philip was in the hospital.

"Hey you," Stephanie interrupted tapping Cassie on the shoulder. "Dancing is about to start in the living room."

"Is it that time already?" Cassie asked looking around.

"Time flies when you're having fun," Stephanie grinned before turning to David. "Hi David, how's Philip doing, when's he coming home?"

"He's good Stephanie, should be home next week."

Cassie frowned at the two of them. How did Stephanie know David?

"Time to dance, you two ready?" Stephanie asked.

Cassie looked at David and smiled. "Would you like to dance?"

"Sure, I'd love to," he replied, and they made their way towards to the living room.

"You coming?" Cassie asked Stephanie over her shoulder.

"Be there in a minute, I've something I need to do first."

Stephanie was up to something. Cassie knew it but the prospect of dancing with David made her drop the subject. The music was soft and inviting as they stepped into the living room. Couples were arm in arm, shuffling around the floor. Wham's *Last Christmas* began playing and David turned to

Cassie.

"You ready?" he asked.

"Yes," she said placing her hand in his.

The touch of his skin sent shockwaves through her body. She hadn't felt this kind of attraction in a long time. Not since Ben, she thought and quickly chastised herself. She wasn't going to let him ruin tonight.

David pulled her in close and together they began to move to the music. They were both silent, caught up in their own little worlds. Cassie smiled. She felt happy and at peace. Stephanie was right, the party was just what she needed. She watched her neighbors and friends smiling and laughing, and she realized that she'd always loved this time of the year. It was magical and everyone embraced the good tidings and Christmas cheer. As they twirled around her living room Cassie allowed her head to rest on David's shoulder. The soft scent of citrus body wash mixed with the scent of mince pies and pine needles filled her nostrils. The music stopped too soon, and she felt herself sigh.

"Thanks for the dance," she whispered as they moved apart.

"It was my pleasure," David smiled, "and I'd love the chance to do it again."

Cassie smiled back. "I'd like that too."

She spotted Stephanie waving to them across the hallway and excused herself.

"You look like you're having a good time," Stephanie beamed.

"I am, thank you, and you were right, this party was just what I needed."

"I'm always right," Stephanie replied handing Cassie a glass of wine. "So, what's he like, David?"

"He's really nice and," Cassie paused.

"Drop dead gorgeous," Stephanie finished, and they both laughed.

"Pity you never found your grandmother's mistletoe, you could have found out a lot more." Stephanie winked at Cassie before excusing herself to go and find Jake and Melissa.

Cassie stood and thought about the mistletoe in the bottom of the decorations box. She could retrieve it, but how would she hang it without anyone seeing? She shrugged her shoulders. There was no way to do it. She had missed her chance because of Ben. She cursed him under her breath. He'd taken everything from her and now he'd taken her chance to kiss David too.

Cassie mingled for the next little while catching up on town news and playing the perfect hostess. She had to admit, the house looked amazing. The lights shone, and the ornaments created the perfect atmosphere. Ivy House was perfect. She'd caught David's eyes a few times and smiled. He was gorgeous.

"There you are," Stephanie exclaimed tapping her on the shoulder. "It's time for the Christmas toast."

"Already?" Cassie said looking at her watch. "God, the time flew."

"Yes, everyone's gathering in the living room, so come on."

They made their way through the crowd and Cassie stood in front of the large, glowing Christmas tree ready to thank her guests and wish them a merry Christmas. It was a tradition. Each year the party host toasted the town and wished for a prosperous holiday season and forthcoming year.

Cassie cleared her throat and asked everyone to raise their glasses.

"Thank you all for coming to Ivy House this year. It's been my pleasure to be your host and I wish every one of you a happy Christmas and prosperous New Year. To us all," she said as she raised her glass.

"To us all," the guests cheered.

She didn't see David in the crowd. In fact, she hadn't seen him in a while. She hoped he hadn't left. She looked around and spotted him standing with Jack and Melissa at the entrance hall. She started to make her way over. She wanted to say goodbye before he left.

"Where are you going?" Stephanie asked smirking at Cassie. "I think someone's caught your attention."

Cassie blushed, "I want to say goodbye to Jake and Melissa before they leave," she lied.

"Cassie Blake, you always were a bad liar," Stephanie laughed. "Come on," she said linking their arms and guiding Cassie across the room. "I've a surprise for you."

Cassie looked at Stephanie. Her surprises never went well.

"What are you up to?"

"You'll see," Stephanie replied tapping the side of her nose. The sign for Cassie to mind her own business.

As they approached Jake and Melissa Cassie's gaze met David's and she smiled. She'd only met him a couple of hours ago but there was something about him, a charm, and a magnetic pull that she hadn't felt in a long time. If she was honest, she didn't want the night to end. She'd enjoyed chatting with him and laughing. He was so easy to talk to.

"Earth to Cassie," Stephanie said pulling her from her thoughts.

Cassie blushed.

"I was just telling Jake and Melissa that we should go out before they head back to the city."

"Yes, we must," Cassie said regaining her composure and looking at David once more. She wondered if she should ask him to come along, but didn't get the chance because Stephanie beat her to it. She was delighted when he said yes.

The guests started leaving and Cassie excused herself.

"I'll be back in a minute."

Cassie thanked her guests as they left, watching out of the corner of her eye to make sure David was still there. When everyone was gone, she made her way back over. She still couldn't believe how well the night had gone and even though she dreaded the clean-up she faced in the morning she couldn't help but smile.

"You're looking very happy," Stephanie said catching her off guard. "The others are getting ready to leave, but I thought you might want to say goodbye to David, so I said I'd go find you."

Cassie smiled at her friend. "Where did you come from? I thought you were with the others?"

"I was, I just had to grab something upstairs. Come on or they'll be gone." Stephanie said pulling Cassie towards the living room.

Jake and Melissa had settled on one of the sofas and David was standing by the Christmas tree admiring the ornaments.

"Go get him," Stephanie whispered in Cassie's ear as she pushed her forward.

Cassie moved into the room and David turned and smiled at her. He had such a beautiful smile, she could look at his face forever.

"I've had a wonderful evening," he said as she got nearer. "Thank you for making me feel so welcome and for the dance."

Cassie felt her face blush as she looked into his deep blue eyes.

"It was my pleasure."

Jake and Melissa stood just then. "We're off now Cass," Jake said. "We'll see you during the week."

"Sorry," Cassie mouthed to David as she turned to see off her guests.

"I have to go too," he said and followed.

"Not so fast, you two," Stephanie said stopping them at the living room door.

They both stopped, a look of confusion on their faces.

"Look up, it's tradition you know," Stephanie said beaming.

Cassie looked up and gasped. Her grandmother's mistletoe was hanging just where it always had been.

"But how?" she asked

"The bottom of the box," Stephanie replied winking at her. "Now go on, you have to or it's bad luck."

Cassie blushed and looked at David. He looked nervous.

"It's okay if you don't want to," she whispered stepping closer to him.

She watched him swallow deeply, his Adam's apple bobbing in his throat. He moved closer too and looked deep into her eyes before touching his soft luscious lips to hers. Her breath left her and her heart pounded in her chest. It was the best kiss she'd ever had, and she wanted so much to deepen it.

David pulled back and smiled. "I've wondered how your lips tasted for five years."

Cassie looked at him, a stunned expression on her face.

"It was worth the wait," he grinned.

"But, I don't understand," she fumbled.

"I was here, five years ago. I watched you all night waiting for the chance to get you under this mistletoe and just when I had some idiot bumped into me and fell. You caught him and then well," he shrugged, "you know the rest."

"Ben," was all Cassie could say. She remembered how he'd

fallen right into her under the mistletoe and how she'd taken it as a sign that he was the one. If only she'd seen David that night. She would have known.

"I'm sorry," was all she could say.

"I'm not, that kiss was worth waiting for and I hope there'll be many more."

Cassie took in a deep breath. She'd been wrong about grandma's mistletoe. It did work, and it did bring true love. It had brought David to her five years ago, but she'd been too blind to see.

"I'd like that very much," she smiled at David before looking up at the mistletoe. Thank you, grandma, you've brought me my magic.

The End

# FINDING FOREVER